Date Due

THE GIRL MOST LIKELY
TO BE LOVED

I wanted to walk in the park with Devon again, hand in hand. I wanted to be his steady girl, his steady, *quiet* girl. I wanted him to kiss me again.

Right then he probably thought of me as the girl who got into noisy debates over everything. Teddy Gideon, the girl most likely to give someone a nervous tic.

Devon said good-bye, and I closed the door behind me. If I hadn't promised myself that I was going to change my life—to become a gentle, smiling girl who whispered in corners and needed sheltering—I would have slammed the door so hard it would have fallen off its hinges!

Other Avon Flare Books by
Jean Thesman

COULDN'T I START OVER?
THE LAST APRIL DANCERS
WAS IT SOMETHING I SAID?

Coming Soon

The Whitney Cousins Trilogy
HEATHER
AMELIA
ERIN

WHO SAID LIFE IS FAIR?

JEAN THESMAN

AN AVON FLARE BOOK

AVON BOOKS
A division of
The Hearst Corporation
105 Madison Avenue
New York, New York 10016

Copyright © 1987 by Jean Thesman
Published by arrangement with the author
Library of Congress Catalog Card Number: 86-91016
ISBN: 0-380-75088-0
RL: 5.0

First Avon Flare Printing: January 1987

AVON FLARE TRADEMARK REG. U.S. PAT. OFF. AND IN OTHER COUNTRIES, MARCA REGISTRADA, HECHO EN CANADA

Printed in Canada

UNV 10 9 8 7 6 5 4

To Rebecca & Company

Chapter One

IF ANYBODY EVER asks me: "Teddy Gideon, what was the worst time of your life?"—I won't have any trouble remembering.

"It began on a Monday," I'll say, "in the second week of my junior year at Catherwood High. Things started out Bad, went immediately to Disaster, and everything galloped downhill from there."

To begin with, I slept through my alarm that Monday morning, and I didn't wake up until I smelled something awful, which meant Mom was fixing breakfast. She was in her "natural foods" phase then. By the time I showered, dressed, and staggered downstairs under a load of half-done homework, this awful goop on the stove was making horrible burbling, sucking noises and turning gray.

Mom was stirring it while she read a new occult thriller, and that explains a lot. Also, she was humming and smiling, a sure sign that whatever she put in my lunch bag that day would make my feet grow even bigger.

I reminded myself to forget my lunch, and I was just about to sit down at the table when the phone rang.

"Get that, will you?" Mom asked. "I'm at a really good part." She was smacking her lips over the book. Believe me, nobody would have smacked her lips over what was in the pot.

Lucie Drake was on the line. She was editor of the high school paper, a gorgeous senior, and a friend of mine since

1

I became feature editor. Usually she spoke in the cool, calm way I had always envied, but this time she sounded mad.

"Teddy," she said, "be sure to meet me in the *Gazette* office before first class. Get there as soon as you can."

"What's up?" I asked, noting dismally that Mom had put aside her book and was shoveling sticky gray junk into a bowl. Dominic, our big dumb dog, slithered out of the room. I guess he was afraid the bowl was for him, but I knew better.

Lucie was blowing her nose furiously, so I knew she was bent out of shape. Everyone who knew her could usually tell when Lucie was upset because her allergies got worse.

"Mr. Trumpteller just called me. He wants the kids who work on the *Gazette* to meet with him during first period, but I want to talk to you before that."

Only Lucie called the new principal by his real name. The rest of us called him "Trumpet," because he talked too much. Maybe he was nervous, trying to take the place of the old principal—a man everybody liked.

"What does Trumpet want?" I asked suspiciously while I picked a bit of fuzz off my new yellow shirt.

"I don't have time to fill you in now. I've got to call the others. But you get to school quickly. And don't tell anybody anything until I talk to you first."

"Tell anybody *what?*" I squalled into the phone, but Lucie had hung up.

"What was all that about?" Mom stopped reading her book and put down her carrot juice.

"Lucie's called a special meeting for the *Gazette* staff." I grabbed my coat from the hook by the door. "Did Dad leave already? I don't have time to eat, and I need a ride to school."

"Of course he's left. He had a breakfast meeting with someone."

2

Breakfast meeting, my eye. He'd smelled the gray stuff, too. Dominic was scratching on the back door, pleading to be let out before Mom remembered him and scraped some of that glop into his pan. I let him out as I left, calling my good-byes to Mom as I slammed the door behind us. Of course I remembered to forget the neat brown sack containing my lunch. Ugh. There's only so much a girl can take in one morning.

Dominic wagged his tail guiltily as he crawled under the porch, and I hurried through the gate. Rain falls in Washington State a lot more than we like to admit, and it started up again before I had gone a block. I had forgotten my umbrella in my rush, and my long brown hair was sure to be soaked by the time I ran the six blocks to school, but with any luck at all, Jo-Sue's little hair dryer would be in our locker. I could make some quick repairs in the *Gazette* office while Lucie was filling me in on the big news.

A bad start, right? It got worse.

I was about two blocks from school, splashing through the puddles, when I saw Devon Tracy coming along the street that intersected mine from the east. Oh, joy! I thought. We'll get to the corner at the same time and he'll have to walk with me. Opportunities like that don't come along too often.

Devon was new in Catherwood. Tall, with dark brown hair, he had wonderful eyes that were so dark they looked black. He also had this funny, crooked grin that gave me shivers. Yum-yum, you say? He didn't know I was alive. Not yet, anyway. But I had all kinds of plans for the two of us because he was the first boy I'd ever met who kept popping up in my dreams. Oh, I'd been interested in boys before, but if you've seen the same guys day in and day out since your swing-set days, they don't seem all that romantic. Devon was different.

I slowed my pace a little to time our meeting just right.

He was looking down and hadn't seen me yet, and my heart was beating so hard I thought I was going to faint.

"Hey, Teddy!"

Oh, no, I couldn't believe it! Coming from the other direction was Billy McGill.

Ordinarily, I would have been glad to see Billy. After all, he had defended me in kindergarten when the other kids teased me about my name, and he'd been my self-appointed knight in shining armor ever since. But on that particular morning, I didn't want Billy walking with me and giving certain people the wrong ideas.

He always had this sort of haunted smile and a way of touching my hair that let everybody know he had a crush on me. What would happen if Devon thought the feeling was mutual? That didn't fit in with my plans.

But all was lost. Devon looked up when he heard Billy call my name, then put his head down against the rain again and zipped around the corner. Billy loped across the street and caught up with me. He hadn't even noticed Devon.

The rain had made his blond curly hair even curlier. Incredibly long lashes blinked sleepily over his hazel eyes. Billy was sweet. And he was always and forever an out-sider, so I worried about him sometimes. But not that day.

"Good morning, Billy." I sighed. "How come you're showing up at school before second period?"

He shrugged without answering. Billy wasn't much of a talker. Falling into step with me, he automatically took my books and slung them under his arm. He looked at me, and I looked ahead at Devon's back, now a block ahead of us.

Right then I knew that I was going to have to do something about Billy, and soon, because things were getting out of hand. I didn't feel about him the way I knew he felt about me. He'd been my shadow for years, and even Jo-Sue, who isn't the most perceptive person in the world, said she bet Billy actually loved me and wasn't I going to do something about it before everybody began to think it was okay with me.

One last look at Devon's back before he was lost in the crowd of kids on the school steps convinced me that this was as good a time as any to "do something" about Billy.

I took a deep breath and shoved back my wet bangs. "Billy," I began.

But he interrupted me. "Your eyes look green today instead of blue." He cleared his throat suddenly. "Will you go to a movie with me tonight?"

He just blurted it out and then looked away quickly. My heart sank to my big feet. After all these years of trailing me around, he finally got to the point of actually asking me for a real date, and it was at the same moment that I was going to tell him I could like him only as a friend. There were times when I would have been glad to date Billy as a pal. But not now.

But I was saved. "I can't," I said truthfully. "We're going to Grandma's tonight. It's her birthday."

"That's okay." Billy looked away, but not before I saw that he was blushing. Honestly, he was so darned cute. Why did he have to be such a loner? I liked having people around, and even though Billy was almost like a brother, I couldn't understand why he thought that three people sitting together at a lunch table constituted a riot.

Billy slouched off before I could say anything more to him. Then I remembered Lucie and her big news, so I ran up the steps, saying "Hi" to people and smiling and shoving Billy out of my mind again so I wouldn't ruin the rest of the day by being depressed because I couldn't love someone who loved me. So far, Monday didn't look very promising. My plans for Devon had fallen through, Billy caught me off-guard, and I wasn't anxious to talk to Trumpet about anything. I probably looked awful, too.

I should have gone home, eaten the gray glop, and died.

5

Chapter Two

"WHERE HAVE YOU been?" Lucie demanded when I opened the door to the messy room the *Catherwood High Gazette* staff used as an office.

Her usually neat, straight dark hair was mussed, and her big brown eyes bored holes right through me. She was sitting behind the splintered old desk under a sign that said, EDITOR AND BIG BOSS. The rest of us used the long table in the middle of the room.

"Listen," I complained. "I rushed out without even eating breakfast." I'd stopped by my locker and borrowed Jo-Sue's dryer, and now I dumped my books on the table and plugged the dryer into the wall outlet.

"Never mind your hair. We've got a disaster on our hands."

"What disaster?" Frankly, I was more worried about my shoes at that moment than I was about Lucie's problem. They were so wet they squeaked, and I wondered what would happen if I turned the hair dryer on them.

"Mr. Trumpteller wants us to include a special article in the *Gazette.* He and Steve had a big fight about it, and Steve quit."

I gaped at Lucie. Steve was the general news editor and did all the front-page stuff. He'd have been the next general editor after Lucie graduated.

"Steve did what?" I asked, unable to take in what she was saying.

6

"He quit. He told me this morning when I called him. Mr. Trumpteller wanted him to cover the first Student Justice Committee meeting and write at least two columns on it."

"What Student Justice Committee meeting?" I yelled. "I've never heard of a Student Justice Committee meeting, and there's practically nothing going on in this school that I don't know about."

"It's one of Mr. Trumpteller's ideas about solving the discipline problems here."

"What discipline problems?" I asked, trying to be patient. "Does he mean when last year's Pep Club people toilet-papered this year's Pep Club lockers?"

Lucie grinned, remembering the incident on the first day of school. "That, too. But mostly he means the vandalism in the parking lot."

I sank back in my chair. Oh, so that awful business had come up again. Every once in a while, for the last year or so, someone would mess around with the cars in the student parking lot. Smashed eggs on the windshields, that sort of stuff. Once, one of the cars had been broken into and a tape deck stolen. We never did find out who did it, but that was nearly a year before, and how did old Trumpet find out, anyway?

"Give it to me straight," I groaned. "I can take it. What is a Student Justice Committee, and how will it stop the crime wave at Catherwood High?"

Lucie sighed. "Once a month, the class presidents will get together like judges in court. All the kids who have been late to class or have made a mess in the cafeteria or yelled in the halls will have to appear in this court, be tried, and then be sentenced to spend a certain number of hours in a special study hall that will be open before classes start every morning."

My mouth must have been hanging open. "Oh," I said

7

finally. "What does that have to do with the vandalism in the parking lot?"

"Mr. Trumpteller says that one thing leads to another. Kids who mess around in school are more likely to do stupid things in the parking lot." Lucie looked at her watch. "Where is everybody? I don't want any of you going into that meeting without knowing what's happening. One wrong word, or one not-so-funny joke, and we could be in big trouble. Mr. Trumpteller is very serious about this Student Justice Committee."

I had almost forgotten that the entire staff was supposed to meet with Trumpet during first period.

Suddenly the door banged open and Zack Jefferson, the sports editor, came in, out of breath, with his glasses on crooked and his dark hair as wet as mine. He had a half-eaten breakfast roll in one hand. Zack was always eating, but he never gained weight. Lucky him.

"What's going on?" he demanded. "I just saw Steve in the hall and he told me he quit." He saw me then and sat down across from me, immediately starting in on something else. Zack doesn't have what you call a long attention span.

"Hey, Teddy, what happened to your hair? Never mind, you look great. Listen, I interviewed Devon Tracy on Friday and got some good stuff for this edition. Did you guys know he came in fourth in the county 10K?"

"What's that?" I thought he was talking about some sort of computer, but I was more than willing to learn anything that would bring Devon within reach.

"Devon's a runner," Zack explained, smirking. He knew I hated sports. "The 10K is a race, dimwit."

Lucie wasn't going to let Zack and me change the subject for long. "Pay attention, Zack," she demanded, and then she filled him in on the Trumpteller situation.

"Steve would have been managing editor next year," Zack grouched. His nice, blunt face flushed angrily.

"I guess he wanted to make his point about the Student Justice Committee," I supplied. "He thinks it's a dumb idea, and you know how stubborn Steve can get."

Just then, my two feature writers came in. They were both sophomores and looked enough alike to be twins, even though they weren't related. Lucie and I called them "Sure" and "Fine" because that's about all they ever said to us. Fine handed Lucie a note before she sat down.

Lucie read it, then looked at them strangely. "The kids gave you this?"

"Sure," whispered Sure.

Lucie sighed and blew her nose. "It's from the general news staff. They all quit in support of Steve. That means that we'll have to get the paper out all by ourselves."

The room was so quiet that I could hear the typewriter clicking away in the main office next door.

"Suits me." Zack brushed some crumbs off his shirt, littering my books.

"Oh, you!" I shouted. "You do the whole sports thing yourself, anyway. What about us? Lucie will have to take over the general news. That's a big job."

Lucie pulled another tissue from her box. "You're going to be helping, Teddy. Fine and Sure can write book reviews for the feature page."

"WHAT?" we all screamed.

Lucie shrugged. "That's what Mr. Trumpteller wants: book reviews."

Fine and Sure looked at each other, tossed back their blond hair, and stood up. "Forget it," they said in unison. "We quit." And they left.

"Things are getting interesting," Zack said.

"Sure," Lucie responded, groaning.

"Fine," I added to keep the ball rolling.

Zack got up and headed toward the door. "I gotta go. I'm meeting Devon in the student lounge. See you in Trumpet's office."

He shut the door quietly. For once, the mention of Devon's name hadn't made my heart trip. That was because my heart was in my shoes.

"Lucie," I whispered. "We'll have to put out the paper all by ourselves."

"With Miss Bilky's help," Lucie said. "She won't let us down." Miss Bilky was our journalism teacher and faculty advisor.

"Where is she?" I looked around the room as if Miss Bilky might be hiding in a corner. "She always comes by before first period to see what's new."

We stared at each other. The bell rang for first period, and two doors down the hall, Trumpet was waiting for us in his office.

"I'm going to my history class," I said suddenly. "Just tell Trumpet you couldn't find me. I don't want to hear about his stupid Student Justice Committee."

And where was Miss Bilky? I was beginning to get that awful feeling I get sometimes when something bad is going to happen. I'm not into telling fortunes, but every once in a while goose bumps pop out all over me and I just know the great cosmic bad-luck machine is flying over me again and is about to unload on me. Dad says it's because Mom read spooky books when she was pregnant with me. Mom says it's just common sense. Whatever it is, I pay attention.

"Teddy, if you walk out on me now, I'll never forgive you," Lucie said.

I had never seen her her look so worried, and I was ashamed of myself. "Okay," I said, "I'll go with you. But I'm telling you one thing right now: *I'm* not going to write that Student Justice Committee article. Not with Jo-Sue being junior-class president. Lucie!" I wasn't sure she was even listening to me. Sometimes she didn't. "Jo-Sue is our best old pal. She'll have to be one of the judges. That'll make her a fink, and if you think I'm going to be the one to tell the world, you're crazy."

10

But Lucie just looked at me.

I followed her out of the room, still wondering where Miss Bilky was and still covered with goose bumps. My hair was drying by itself and probably looked like a long, brown mop, but at that moment, hair didn't seem very important.

And just to make things even worse, the great cosmic bad-luck machine zapped me again. There, in the student lounge across the hall, I saw Zack talking earnestly with Devon. Both of them turned around and looked at me.

Devon was so gorgeous, and I had never in my life looked more like Dracula's mother. Or a tall, thin witch, with an armload of books, hair like a fright wig, and size 9 feet.

We marched toward Trumpet's office, and Zack caught up with us just outside the door.

"Hey, Teddy," he whispered, "Devon asked me about you. I told him you were Billy McGill's girl."

Zack's idea of humor was the reason he was the sports editor and I was the feature editor. I wondered what would happen to me if I drove a stake through his heart right then and there. But Lucie was pulling at my arm, so I gave Zack my dirtiest look and turned away.

Trumpet's office door was open and he was sitting behind his desk. Seeing him there reminded me of something Mom had read to me when I was a little girl. It was a story about this awful spider who invited a fly into his parlor for lunch, and guess who was lunch? At that moment, I knew how the fly felt.

Chapter Three

MR. TRUMPTELLER WAS several inches over six feet tall, very thin, and older than my father. I'd already had one conversation with him that year, and I was not anxious for another.

That particular disaster happened on the first day of school. Dominic, my fat, dumb old dog, got out of the fenced yard again—we hadn't yet discovered how this was happening—and sneaked after me to school. I caught a glimpse of him just as I was walking up the driveway to the student parking lot, which is the shortest way to the side door near the *Gazette* office.

The instant Dominic saw me looking at him, he collapsed into a big guilty lump right in the middle of the driveway and rolled on his back. It was not a pretty picture. No one is ever going to want him to star in a TV series about a heroic dog. He is exceedingly timid, shaggy, black, and fat, and it's not always easy to tell which end is which. He is also large. Like maybe one hundred and twenty pounds of lovable stupidity.

And no one took him to obedience training classes, mainly because my father said he would not finance a course where the end result would be a fool leading an idiot around on a leash. Mom asked him if he was talking about himself, since she thought that dog obedience training was cruel and that their daughter (me) was certainly too young to take the responsibility. I was in grade school at the time, but already I knew better than to get mixed up in one of their goofy "discussions."

So when I tried to get Dominic to his feet by yelling "Heel!" and "Up!" and various other things, nothing happened except that a small crowd gathered to cheer Dominic on and laugh at me.

Just then, a big black car came roaring around the corner, heading right toward Dominic. If Billy hadn't leaped out of the crowd and shoved Dominic out of the way, Trumpet and his hearse would have killed him.

"You nearly hit my dog!" I yelled.

I was really mad. First of all, he was driving too fast. And he was also in the wrong lane. Furthermore, no one could say that Dominic wasn't a highly visible dog. So I ran after the big black car, not caring one bit about who was driving it, and out hopped this tall, thin man, our new principal. But I didn't know that yet.

He didn't even wait to hear what I had to say. "What's your name?" he asked, all red-faced and huffy.

"Teddy Gideon," I shouted. "Where did you learn to drive?" The kids standing around watching grumbled along with me, saying "Yeah!" and "Where did you learn to drive, mister?"

Billy ambled up then, scowling. "Visitors aren't supposed to park in the student parking lot."

"I'm not a visitor. I'm the principal."

Everybody but Billy, Dominic, and me vanished instantly.

"Staff people aren't supposed to park in the student lot," Billy argued. He liked contradicting teachers and principals. It was a game to him, but I was getting scared for both of us.

"Go to your class," Trumpet said coldly to Billy, and that's how *their* interesting relationship began. It never improved.

I took Dominic home and got back to school late for my first class. What a terrific beginning.

Now here I was, face-to-face with Trumpet again, and I could tell from his expression that he regretted it as much as I did. "I remember you and your dog," he said, and he drummed his long fingers on his desk. "Dogs don't belong on school grounds. They're not trustworthy."

Lucie spoke up quickly before I could protest this insult to Dominic. "You wanted to see the *Gazette* staff this morning, Mr. Trumpteller."

His eyes didn't leave mine. "What's your name again, young lady?"

"Teddy," I replied weakly.

"Is that some sort of nickname?"

I shook my head. I wasn't about to explain that my father named me Theodora for his grandmother, who was arrested when she chained herself to the front door of city hall because she wasn't allowed to vote. Dad is very big on getting involved. Mom took pity on me and had Theodora changed to Teddy as a compromise. I was too young to have an opinion.

"Mr. Trumpteller," Lucie began bravely, but she didn't get a chance to finish. Another of Trumpet's endearing qualities was that he never let anyone finish a sentence.

"Is this the whole *Gazette* staff? Just the three of you?"

Lucie flushed. "The general news editor quit, and so did his writers. And Teddy's writers quit, too."

Trumpet leaned back in his chair and tapped his long teeth with one bony finger. His gaze fell upon poor Zack, who was trying to hide his six-foot frame behind me.

"Who are you?"

Zack explained who he was and what he did, but Trumpet was not impressed.

"The sports page could be jazzed up, son," he barked.

"Jazzed up?" Zack repeated, and his voice cracked.

But Trumpet had finished with him. He shifted his gaze back to me. "Who does the cartoons on the feature page?"

I froze. Trumpet picked up an old copy of the *Gazette* already turned to the feature page and thrust it at me. "This cartoon, for instance. Who drew it? It's not signed. There's only a little animal drawn in the lower corner."

Our eyes locked, and the light finally dawned on him. "I see. It's a teddy bear," he said. "I should have known. You like satire, do you? Some of these cartoons seem a little too controversial. I wonder if that's such a good idea."

I felt Lucie's hand slip around mine and squeeze. She was signaling me to shut up and let her handle this, which was an easy thing to do, because I was so panicked that I couldn't talk.

"Teddy's been doing the cartoons since the last half of her freshman year," she explained. "The *Gazette* won a state prize last year because of one of them. It was reprinted in several newspapers."

Trumpet's eyes never left mine. I think he was having trouble believing that I could contribute anything meaningful to the paper. Finally, he sighed and closed his eyes for a moment. I was sure he was wishing I'd disappear. When I didn't, he abandoned himself to his fate and pawed through a mess of papers on his desk, pulling out several sheets of paper stapled together. "These are your guidelines for the article on the Student Justice Committee. This is a serious subject, so treat it accordingly." The last remark was meant for me. He handed us the papers and gave me a brisk nod.

Zack and I backed away, but Lucie stood her ground. "We have to have all our copy ready for the printer by Wednesday afternoon. That gives us only a couple of days, and there are just three of us now...."

Trumpet's fingers began tapping on the desk again. His pale brown eyes didn't blink. "I feel confident that you will manage," he said.

Lucie pulled a tissue out of her pocket and blew her

nose. Her allergies must have been close to terminal by then. "I guess Miss Bilky will help us get the paper out," she muttered, more to herself than anyone else.

"Miss Bilky," said Trumpet, "is in the hospital. She broke her ankle." He smiled, and I wasn't sure if he was pleased that Miss Bilky had broken her ankle or pleased that we wouldn't be getting any help from her.

Lucie blew her nose again. "Then I guess we'll do our best." The three of us backed toward the door.

"Please shut the door," Trumpet said. Zack shut the door.

We had forgotten to ask for admission slips to our classes, but we weren't going to go back into Trumpet's office. Who could tell what he'd think up next? Now we were late, depressed, and in big trouble.

"What are we going to do?" Zack asked Lucie.

"Give me a break, Zack!" Lucie cried. "Ask me at lunch, when I've had a chance to think." She eyed me then. "You're going to have to get the twins back."

"They don't want to do book reports."

"So *you* do the book reports and give them something else. At least for the time being."

What was the use? I shrugged and dragged myself down the hall toward my history class. With no admission slip and my homework half done, I didn't expect any sort of welcoming committee. At that point, I didn't care that Devon was in that class. I didn't even care that my hair, which is my best feature, looked like Dominic's bed.

The class was taking a surprise quiz when I walked in. The teacher gave me a copy of the test and a dirty look, and I slouched to my seat. Devon didn't even glance up. Across the room, Jo-Sue wiggled her eyebrows at me, and I wondered if she had heard that she and the other class presidents were being set up for a Fink-of-the-Year contest. Probably not, since she was still smiling.

I finished the test before the bell rang and sneaked a

16

look at the papers Trumpet had given us. Good grief. We'd have to change the name of the *Gazette* to the *Catherwood High Bird-Cage Liner.* Nobody was going to enjoy reading about that dumb Student Justice Committee.

Jo-Sue was late getting to the cafeteria at lunchtime. Lucie and I were sharing a small pizza when Jo-Sue slammed her books down on the table.

"Have you two heard about the Student Justice Committee?" she asked.

"Have you?" Lucie countered.

"Trumpet pulled me out of my last class to tell me. Do you believe that this is happening?"

We shook our heads, and Jo-Sue sat down with a thump. I could tell she was upset even before she threw her books down, because her short curly hair had been pulled into funny little blond peaks all over her head. Whenever she's out of sorts, Jo-Sue pulls her hair. Lucie blows her nose. And I fuss and complain. And all three of us eat.

"Save my place," Jo-Sue said. "I'm going to get pizza, too. It looks good today. Can I get you two anything else?"

Could she! Lucie and I had built up such huge nervous appetites that we decided Jo-Sue couldn't carry enough to satisfy us, so we all went back to the counter and ordered more of everything in sight.

After all, life has to go on.

Chapter Four

I DIDN'T LEAVE school until close to dinnertime that day. After our last class, Lucie, Zack, and I got together in the *Gazette* office to compare notes. I had bribed the twins into coming back to work by promising them that I would do the book reviews and that they could start right out doing a funny article on the girls' gym for the first edition.

Zack, it turned out, had been doing some serious thinking, and that was unusual for him.

"I'll go see Miss Bilky at the hospital tonight and find out when she's coming back," he told us. "The librarian knows where she is. And what's more, the librarian helped with a school paper once, so she said she'd do what she could to give us a hand until Miss Bilky gets back."

Miss Lamb, the librarian, was a neat lady. Maybe there was hope for us after all. I sat a little straighter, and Lucie stopped blowing her nose long enough to smile.

"And," Zack said with a big grin, "I think I found more help."

"Who?" Lucie asked quickly.

"Or what?" At that point, I was ready to assign work to Dominic.

"Are you ready for this, Teddy?" Zack was strutting around the office with his thumbs hooked in his belt. There were times when Zack actually seemed almost attractive, but this wasn't one of them.

"Get on with it," Lucie said with a groan.

"I've got a recruit for the paper."

Lucie put her head down on her desk. "We don't need any more sportswriters, Zack. We need people for the general news."

"So he's willing to do general news." Zack was getting huffy.

"Can he spell?" I asked suspiciously. Lots of kids wanted to work on the paper, but most of them couldn't spell.

"Of course he can spell! And he's worked on a paper before." Zack took off his glasses and peered at them. "No wonder I thought I was going blind," he said, and then he disgusted Lucie and me by spitting on his lenses and rubbing them on his shirt.

"Gee, Zack, I hope he has half your charm," I said. "Why don't you get contact lenses like everybody else?"

Zack blinked and looked pained. "I had contact lenses; I kept losing them. Now will you quit nagging and listen to me?"

"So who is this new guy?" Lucie's scowl was warning Zack to take care.

"Devon Tracy." Zack shoved his glasses back on and resumed his strutting. "What do you think of *that*, Teddy?"

Automatically, my hand went to my hair. "You'd better not be kidding around."

"I'm not kidding! Do I look like I'm kidding?"

Lucie stared first at me and then at Zack. "Am I supposed to be impressed by that name? Who is this Devon Tracy?"

I hadn't told Lucie, or anyone, that Devon was on my mind most of the time. Zack, who had some sort of sixth sense—and more curiosity than was good for him—had figured it out.

"Oh, Devon's new this year; he's a junior," I said feebly. My face was red.

"He's turning out for track. He'll be the best runner we

19

have," Zack supplied. "He has a free period, so he's going to sign up for journalism."

Lucie lost interest. "Jocks can't spell. If you hired him, you get to fire him."

"He can spell! What is it with you, Lucie? The guy can spell, and he's even been on the honor roll. What more do you want?"

"He sounds like a big brag to me." Lucie stared at me again. "You look like you're going into orbit."

"Wait until you see him."

"Cute?"

I nodded soberly.

"Aw, you two make me sick!" Zack shouted. "'Is he cute?'" he mimicked. "'Can he dance?' 'Does he have his own car?' Don't you ever pay any attention to the things that are really important?" When he left, he slammed the door behind him so hard that the windows rattled.

"I'm going to pretend I didn't hear that," Lucie said.

"Me, too."

She examined her fingernails and sighed. "Why am I so lucky? Now we have an athlete for the general news page. He's *new* in school. How come I have the feeling that my troubles are just beginning?"

I didn't say anything to her at that point. She'd just have to wait and see Devon for herself. But things were beginning to look up a bit. If he worked on the *Gazette,* we'd be spending lots of time together, and who knew what might happen?

Lucie and I started to work on the article about the Student Justice Committee, following Trumpet's guidelines. The twins came in for a while to sympathize and gloat. They were sorry that Steve and his staff had quit, of course, but they'd both been given small promotions, too.

Then it was time to leave. Lucie's boyfriend, Mark, came by for her, and the twins took off with another girl. I was looking forward to walking home alone, just to quiet my nerves. Usually, life wasn't that hectic around Catherwood High.

The rain had stopped, and the streets were clean and shining in the late afternoon light. The air smelled wonderful—part damp trees and part late-summer roses. I inhaled deeply and started through the parking lot.

Silently, like a shadow, Billy slipped out from between two cars and joined me.

"I didn't know you were waiting for me," I said. Billy often waited for me, but usually during the day he told me he would.

He shrugged and fell into step with me. "You're going to be late getting to your grandmother's."

I had forgotten about Gram's birthday dinner, but there was still plenty of time to get ready. "We don't leave until six."

Billy watched his feet while he walked, a sure sign that something was on his mind. His blond hair fell over his face, and he looked much younger than sixteen. We have the same birthday, and it was Billy who gave me Dominic at our joint eighth birthday party.

"I heard that there's all kinds of trouble on the *Gazette*," he said.

I sighed. "Oh, we're getting it straightened out."

"I heard that there's going to be some sort of court thing at school. Trials and punishment." Billy was smiling that odd, wonderful half-smile of his, and you'd have thought the Student Justice Committee was nothing more than a small fuss in an anthill.

I wanted to reach out and hug Billy then. If anyone was going to be thrown into the jaws of the Student Justice Committee, it was likely to be Billy. He was nearly always late to school and only did homework when he was in the mood, which was practically never. He was one of the best students in our grade school, but after his mother died, he

21

got to be a little strange. Both he and his brother, Cal, changed.

The moment Cal crossed my mind, I looked back over my shoulder. As Billy shadowed me, Cal always shadowed Billy. He was a lot younger than Billy—still in junior high —and he idolized his big brother. Usually, he was just a few steps behind us when we were walking home, a surly, scowling boy who never said anything much to anyone.

"I don't see Cal," I said to Billy.

Billy looked around, surprised. "He was here a few minutes ago. I guess he took off when you came out."

Cal and I weren't friends. In fact, there were times when I would have liked to sock that kid. But I tried to understand that his mother's death must have been even worse for him than it was for Billy. I remembered Mrs. McGill a little. She was sweet and quiet, like Billy, and she just kept getting sweeter and quieter, until one night she died in her sleep of some sort of heart trouble. Thinking about her brought a lump to my throat.

Billy had a paperback book stuffed in his jacket pocket. He read more books than anyone I knew, except my parents.

"What are you reading?" I asked.

He pulled the book out of his pocket. "It's a science fiction anthology. I'm done with it now, so I thought I'd give it to your dad. I don't think he has this one."

Billy had probably read the whole book during classes that day. Trumpet was going to have a wonderful time trying to solve his problems with Billy. I wasn't so sure he could win. Billy was . . . well, his own self.

When we got to my house, Dominic met Billy at the door and leaped around like a demented water buffalo. Billy hugged the dog, gave the book to Dad, and smiled at Mom. He was always welcome at our house, but he seldom stayed more than a few minutes, now that we were too old to play on the swing set. Sometimes I wished those days weren't over. Everything seemed to be simple then.

"Wish Gram a happy birthday for me," Billy said. I could see that Mom and Dad were just about to ask him to go with us, but Billy eased himself out the door and shut it softly behind him.

Dominic lumbered slowly and sadly to the kitchen and scratched on the back door to be let out. I expected that he would crawl under the porch as usual and console himself by gnawing on the log he dragged under there the year before.

"How's Billy doing in school?" Dad demanded of me, as if I were responsible for Billy's failures.

I shrugged as easily as Billy would have. "You'll have to ask him, if you really think that it's our business."

"She's got you there." Mom was grinning.

"You can't help Billy by covering up for him," Dad said, favoring both of us with a grumpy look.

"You can't help him by butting into his personal business, either." Mom could always top Dad when the subject of Billy came up. She thought he was so unique he should be made a national monument. Dad thought Billy needed help.

Dad gave up and stomped off to his den, holding Billy's book in his eager paw, obviously glad to be at quits with us.

"We're leaving in half an hour," Mom called after him.

"I'm *already* ready!" he shouted.

Just then the doorbell rang. I answered it, thinking that perhaps Billy had come back.

But it was the woman who lived next door. Dad called her "Mrs. Dimwitly," although that wasn't her name. He said she looked like a Dimwitly to him. When we asked him what a Dimwitly looked like, he said, "Trouble."

Her fat, blotchy face was red with agitation. "Your awful dog is dead out on the sidewalk."

23

I sighed pointedly. Dominic was not dead. We had been through this before with Mrs. Dimwitly, who'd hated him since he was a puppy and he piddled on her porch once when she yelled at him and scared him.

Dominic must have sneaked out of the fenced backyard again—how he did it was a mystery to us—and his favorite place to sulk was right in front of the house, where everyone could see him. He was too cheerful to sulk very long, and he usually fell asleep within a minute. On his back. I must admit that Dominic could look quite deceased at times.

"I'll get him," I said as I brushed past Mrs. Dimwitly.

"You'd better keep that bad dog in your yard." She followed me down the steps. "I don't like that dog. He's too big. He could be dangerous."

We stood beside Dominic, who did indeed look dead. I poked him with the toe of my sneaker and he groaned.

"Get up, you idiot."

He shoved himself up to his feet, with lots of grunts and sighs, and staggered up the steps. He wasn't too fond of Mrs. D., so he didn't wag his tail as he passed her.

"You're going to have to keep that dog in your yard," she repeated.

"Right." I went up the steps after Dominic. Mom was holding the door open for us.

"If he gets out again, I don't know what's going to happen."

"Right." I slipped through the door, and Mom closed it behind me. Dominic was already asleep again, blocking the door to the dining room.

"How on earth does that big moose get out?" Mom asked.

"Who knows? He's too fat and old to jump the fence. And he's not smart enough to open the latch on the gate." Dominic's escapes worried me. But foolish as he was, he wasn't foolish enough to let us see how he was managing this magic act of his.

Mom took her jacket off the back of a chair. "That woman has not spoken one word to me for six years. Not since the day your father had that fence put up and cut off her view through our kitchen window."

"I hope you're not complaining," I said. "I wish she wouldn't speak to me. Do you want me to tell Dad we're ready to go?"

"Sure. You get him out of his cave, and I'll get the car out of the garage."

Dominic sighed deeply in his sleep, and I patted him once before I went upstairs for Dad. Maybe the dog was dreaming of Billy. He didn't know Devon. Not yet.

Chapter Five

THE RAIN HAD stopped by the next morning, and the sun was shining when I got up. Weather like that fools us into thinking that September is an extension of summer, and I always fall for the joke, even though I know better. I put on a thin cotton shirt and a denim skirt and went downstairs to find that Dad had fixed bacon and eggs for breakfast. Even Dominic was interested enough to lean against a table leg and moan hopefully whenever Dad looked at him. Mom was gnawing on something that looked like a shingle and reading a cheery paperback about mass murder.

I almost asked Dad to give me a ride to school, but then I remembered Devon, so I figured that if I timed everything right, I could end up at the same intersection where I'd seen him on the morning of That Day, and maybe he'd walk the rest of the way to school with me.

In spite of everything, I was still trying to keep control over my destiny. Every girl fantasizes about having a steady boyfriend by her junior year in high school, and I wanted Devon to be mine. Those wonderful black eyes and that magic smile never seemed to be out of my mind.

So I'd walk.

"Want a ride to school?" Dad asked, probably reading my mind.

"I need exercise," I said, stretching to prove my point. "And the sun is out."

Dad stared at me for a moment, then passed the eggs to

me again. Mom glanced up from her book long enough to say that I'd need the exercise to work off all the cholesterol I was consuming. I wolfed down another helping of eggs and bacon, and when I left, Dad was asking Mom how her own mother just celebrated her sixtieth birthday even though she ate eggs every morning.

Mom ignored him, and I closed the door quietly behind me. I didn't even need a jacket that morning, although I brought one along, anyway; I trotted toward school, grinning in anticipation. Devon just had to be there again, and this time I knew of a way to start a conversation with him. We could talk about the *Gazette*.

I was a little late, I guess, because Devon turned the corner while I was still half a block away, but that didn't stop me. I called out his name, and he turned and stopped. And smiled.

"I hear you're joining us on the *Gazette* staff," I panted as I caught up.

"For a while, anyway. Zack can be very persuasive."

What did he mean, "for a while"? That sounded a little uncertain. Well, no matter. Friendships could develop in minutes, I knew. And I wanted to give this friendship all the help I could. While I wasn't very experienced with boys, I could tell that Devon hadn't fallen in love with me on the first day of school. But he *had* asked Zack about me, so at least he was interested.

"How long have you worked on the paper?" Devon looked down at me out of the corner of his eye and then smiled suddenly. That wiped anything I had planned to say right out of my mind.

"Since the last half of my freshman year," I croaked. I couldn't think of another word.

"You must like it, then." He smiled again.

"It's fun. You'll see." My mind was so empty that my ears were ringing. Now that I was walking with him, what else could I talk about? We seemed to have exhausted the subject of the *Gazette,* and the paper was one of my favorite things. The silence that had fallen was thick enough to smother me, but Devon didn't seem to be bothered. He just walked along, looking pleased with the whole world. He was wearing a cream-colored sweater that showed off his summer tan, so the whole world had to be pleased with him, too. I certainly was.

Think of something, I ordered myself. Teddy, wake up!

"Did you finish your history assignment?" he asked.

History? I swallowed, trying to remember. I decided that I must have done the assignment and told him I had.

"Good." He glanced sideways down at me again. "So did I."

"Good."

We were getting close to school by then, and I was sure I was ruining any chance I might have to impress him. Who wants to take out a girl who can't think of anything to say? Especially if she has big feet.

"Do you want to have a career in journalism?" he asked, breaking the awful silence.

"What? No," I blurted stupidly, "I'd rather do cartoons."

Well, Teddy, that sounds dumb, I told myself. No, I don't want to be a world-famous journalist. I want to draw pictures. I also want to drop dead.

Devon looked away, then down at the sidewalk. "I was wondering if you might like to see a movie on Friday. It's about a journalist. But maybe . . ."

"I'd love to," I said quickly, but my heart had stopped beating, so I probably wouldn't live until Friday. I couldn't believe my luck. Devon asked me out on a date!

"You sure you won't be bored?" His grin told me he knew the answer before he asked.

"I won't be bored," I assured him. We were crossing the street toward the school then, and I could see Jo-Sue waiting for me in the driveway. She was tugging on her hair, and that was a bad sign. Oh, Jo-Sue, I thought. Couldn't you have your disaster some other time?

"There's Joe-Sue," Devon said. "I guess she's waiting for you, so I'll see you during first period." He turned and crossed the lawn toward the main door.

I stopped and stared after him until Jo-Sue joined me. Was he shy? He hadn't seemed shy to me before. Actually, I thought he seemed cool, really confident. No, he couldn't be shy. He was just sorry he asked me to go out, after he'd had a chance to realize what an idiot I was.

"Did I interrupt something important?" Jo-Sue plucked distractedly at her hair. "Sorry, but I just *had* to talk to you before school. And not near the lockers. I need privacy."

With one last look at Devon trotting up the front steps of the school, I followed Jo-Sue. We walked around the parking lot to the back of the building, and I listened while Jo-Sue talked.

"I can't do this stupid Student Justice Committee thing. The more I think about it, the madder I get. Do you know how bad we're going to look to the rest of the school? Especially since everything that happens during the meetings will end up in the *Gazette,* even the names of the kids who get into trouble."

"Did you get a chance to talk to the other class officers?"

"Sure. We got together at my house last night. Half of them don't care, except for the time it's going to take. The rest don't like it, but we don't know what to do about it."

"What about John?" He was the senior-class president, and Jo-Sue really admired him.

She smiled weakly. "He's with me. He doesn't want to be any part of it. But I don't think he wants to make an issue out of it. And what good would it do? Trumpet isn't going to listen to us."

"When is the first meeting supposed to take place?"

29

"A week from Friday. After that, there'll be one every month."

"Who's going to be turning in the kids? The teachers?" Just thinking about it made me angry all over again.

"Sure. Teachers, janitors, hall monitors, cafeteria workers." Jo-Sue's voice trailed off. "They'll hand out pink demerit slips and give carbon copies to Trumpet."

I scuffed my shoes along the asphalt as I walked. It seemed to help my thinking. "In other words, everybody tattles on everybody else."

"Something like that."

"I know there's going to be a demerit system. But what sort of sentences are you supposed to hand out?"

"Trumpet gave us a list, and each big fat crime has so many demerits. One demerit for each minute you're late to class, and so on. After you collect enough demerits, you start serving hours in the penalty study hall."

"I get the picture." I sighed and scuffed a little harder. "Why doesn't Trumpet do the judging himself? Why drag in the class presidents?"

"He says that this will teach the kids what the adult world is like. He gave each of us a copy of his new rules and a lecture that's about five pages long. All about peer-group pressure and responsibility. Actually, I hate to say it, but it does make a horrible kind of sense. It's just that it's going to make us look bad. And I don't want to be a judge or a cop. Not ever. I want to be the manager of a big hotel."

Jo-Sue looked as if she were ready to cry. "When you're a hotel manager," I told her, "you'll have to supervise security people and tell them to throw guests out if they're too noisy or whatever. Maybe you'll learn something from this experience that will help you make decisions then." I didn't believe this myself.

She glared at me. "Don't be dumb, Teddy. All I'm going to learn from this is how to lose friends. Half the people I

30

know are late to class at least once a day. How many times have *you* been in the halls without a pass? Have you ever thrown a gum wrapper on the lawn?"

She had a point. We should show up to class on time. And I'd thrown gum wrappers and other junk on the lawn more than once. If I had to do penalty time for wandering around the school during class without a hall pass, I'd be spending every morning for the rest of my life in that dumb study hall, with most of my friends for company.

It was right that Trumpet should crack down on us. But it was wrong to ask us to turn each other in.

I looked at my watch. I had exactly five minutes before the first bell, and I hadn't been in the *Gazette* office yet.

"We'll talk about this at lunch," I promised Jo-Sue, and then I ran for the door nearest the office. The sun was still shining, but otherwise I felt as if November had arrived early. A week before, Jo-Sue, Lucie, and I hadn't had a trouble in the world. Now, all three of us had more than we'd ever need to keep us busy.

The only bright spot in my day was the moment when Devon asked me out. I wanted to tell Jo-Sue, but not when she was feeling so down.

Lucie and Zack were in the office, helping Sure and Fine with their first big assignment. When I arrived, they left the twins to muddle along by themselves and pulled me into the corner near Lucie's big old desk.

"I went to see Miss Bilky last night," Zack said. "She's had surgery on her ankle, and she'll be in the hospital for three weeks. She'll have to rest at home for three or four more weeks, so we can't expect much help from her."

Oh, boy, I thought. What next? "What about the librarian, Miss Lamb? You said she'd help."

Zack nodded. "But she doesn't know the routine here. We're really on our own for the first issue."

Lucie shoved some papers at me. "Have a look at this

stuff before lunch. My allergies are affecting my brain. I don't know if the first page is any good or not."

I tucked Lucie's pages into my folder, then handed her mine. "Here's a book review that was left over from my Modern American Lit. class last year. See if this is boring enough to satisfy Trumpet. I don't know what I'm going to do about the gossip column yet—the general news staff always wrote it. And the twins will have to do their article on their own." I raised my voice to make certain they heard me.

"Sure."

"Fine."

"This looks okay." Lucie dropped my book review on her desk. "What about the cartoon? Are you finished yet?"

I had dreamed one up in the middle of the night. "It shows our glorious new principal standing in line with the freshmen, waiting to pay their activity-card fees. He won't mind that."

"I wouldn't bet on it," Zack said. "Do another one, but leave him out. And be sure you get it to me by three tomorrow. No matter what, I'm going to the printer at the regular time."

"Did Miss Bilky tell you what to do?" I asked.

Zack's face flamed. "I already knew what to do! I've been doing it with her for a year!"

I backed off his case. Zack can be the biggest pest in school, but when it comes to the paper, he really does know his stuff. "Okay, okay, I'll do the cartoon over and get it to you tomorrow morning."

We had about thirty seconds before the second bell, so we all ran toward our classrooms. I hadn't had much time to think about Devon's actually asking me out, and I remembered it again briefly as I rushed into class and saw him sitting there, head bent over a book. He looked up at me and grinned, and I had a quick moment to feel thrilled all over.

Then the PA system went on with a burst of static and a high shriek, and Trumpet treated us to his morning announcements. He told us there would be a special assembly during third period, when he would explain his "exciting" new idea—a Student Justice Committee.

The class groaned in unison, and my gaze met Jo-Sue's guiltily. I wondered if she was already feeling like the traitor she was about to become.

Chapter Six

I SAT BETWEEN Zack and Jo-Sue in the back of the auditorium during the special assembly, and we listened attentively to Trumpet's long speech about crime and punishment at Catherwood High.

"Do you believe this guy?" Zack whispered in my ear.

"No, this is a bad dream and I'm going to wake up in a minute and find out that the only thing wrong with me is my mother's fiber pancakes with garlic syrup."

"Barf," Zack mumbled with a moan, and he slid down in his seat. His bright blue eyes blinked behind his glasses.

Jo-Sue scowled at us. "Hush! We're already in enough trouble."

Jo-Sue always got the Good Citizen Awards in grade school, but Zack and I weren't the only ones talking in the auditorium. I'd have bet Trumpet succeeded in keeping the attention of about only ten students. You know the ones I mean—the kids who actually volunteer to be hall monitors. Everyone else was either groaning or laughing, but Trumpet didn't mind. He went on and on, explaining how the Student Justice Committee was going to work, and he left the auditorium while the kids were still booing.

I would have felt sorry for Trumpet if I hadn't hated the idea of a Student Justice Committee so much. Believe me, it hadn't been hard for the *Gazette* staff and class officers to keep the whole mess a secret until he had the chance to make this public announcement.

We went back to our classes, where everybody talked about the principal for five minutes and then forgot all about him. D-Day, the day the demerit system was to begin, was only a few days off. I don't think anyone but the *Gazette* staff and Jo-Sue really believed that it was going to happen. I remember thinking that next Monday was going to be an interesting day, and then the whole thing slipped from my mind. At least temporarily. After all, Devon had asked me to go to a movie with him, and believe me, that was more important. My heart banged against my ribs every time I thought about it.

Zack shot that dream down for me at lunch. With his usual sensitivity, he sat down next to me in the cafeteria and said, "Devon says you're going with us on Friday."

I swallowed the cracker in my mouth. "What do you mean, *us*, cowboy?" I was beginning to feel the cold breeze from the great cosmic bad-luck machine hovering over my head.

Zack grinned. *"Us,* that's what I mean. Did you think Devon had only two passes to the movie?"

"What passes are you talking about?" I demanded. "Have you been standing on your head again?"

Zack took the rest of my crackers and crammed them in his mouth, so I had to wait until he could talk, which he could only do after he finished my soft drink. "Passes," he choked. "Devon's sister got passes to the movie for all of us. We're going to the first showing right after school. Didn't he tell you?"

Devon hadn't had a chance to tell me because that was when we saw Jo-Sue and she wanted to talk. Great. I must have looked like the biggest fool in school, which takes some doing. I punched Zack's arm hard enough to make him wince.

"You ate my lunch, you creep." I wouldn't have dared let him know why I was really angry with him.

But Zack knew he was on to something. "Didn't Devon tell you?" he persisted.

"He was *going* to, but we were interrupted. Go up to the counter and get me something to eat, you pig. After this, buy your own lunch." I was afraid I might start crying, and I needed to come up with something to occupy Zack's tiny brain long enough for him to forget any suspicions he had that I might have been silly enough to think I'd had a date with Devon. Where Zack's concerned, nothing matters more than food.

He trotted off and, while he was gone, Lucie and Jo-Sue showed up. By that time, Lucie had heard about the movie passes too, so I tried to pretend that I was delighted to have the whole *Gazette* staff along, even the twins. Ha. This was no date, it was a convention. How could I have been so dumb?

Zack came back with a salad and a sandwich for me, and he even apologized. Sometimes he can be almost bearable.

But not even food could make me feel better. I had spent a couple of delicious hours thinking that I actually had a date with Devon. I even planned how I was going to tell Jo-Sue about it the first moment we had some privacy and she wasn't talking about her troubles. Actually, and I hate to admit it, I was even planning what I was going to wear.

I got through the rest of the day, and after my last class I hung around the *Gazette* office for a while, helping Lucie and the twins. I paid no attention at all to Zack and Devon, who weren't paying any attention to me either. Finally, I decided I'd had enough, so I said good-bye and left. Alone. I couldn't tell whether Devon liked me or not.

I hadn't seen Billy all day, but I half expected him to be in the parking lot again, and he was. I also caught a glimpse of his little brother, Cal, running down the driveway. When Billy got close enough to hear me, I asked him why Cal was always at the high school instead of four blocks away at the junior high.

"He meets me here after school," Billy said as he took my books. "Some of the kids at his school give him a hard time if they catch him alone."

"That's too bad." I didn't really care because my day had been so awful that I simply didn't have enough energy to feel guilty that I didn't like Cal much. A damp wind was blowing. I was cold and miserable and mad at the whole world.

"So now we know about this Justice Committee thing," Billy said, as if it were happening a thousand miles away and couldn't hurt him.

"Dumb, isn't it?"

Billy shrugged. "School is dumb."

We walked along in silence for a block or so. My mind was on Devon, and I wasn't very good company, but I had never asked Billy to wait for me after school, so I figured that he had to take his chances at being bored with me. But he always had a funny sort of half-smile on his face when he walked with me, and he didn't seem especially unhappy that I wasn't talking.

So Devon hadn't actually asked me out after all. I had been on real dates before, so it wasn't as if Devon would have been the first guy ever to ask me. I'd just never really cared about anyone until Devon came to our school. Of course, I told myself, we hardly knew each other. There was plenty of time.

But I didn't belive that. For me, there was never plenty of time for anything. I always seemed to be in such a hurry. I wanted everything to happen right now! And hardly anything did. At least, not much that was good.

I must have sighed, because Billy asked me what was wrong.

Everything, I wanted to say, but I just shook my head.

And then I caught another quick glimpse of Cal. This

time he was about a block ahead of us, ducking down behind a hedge.

"Darn your brother! I hate it when he sneaks around. Tell him to either walk with us or go home." The moment I said it I was sorry, but Cal could be so hard to take.

Billy made a "go away" gesture the next time Cal's head popped up, but perversely, Cal straightened up and waited for us instead of going home. He studied his feet until I reached him, and then he suddenly looked at me. His eyes were so hot and angry that he almost scared me.

"I wish you'd walk with us, Cal," I complained. "It drives me crazy to have you popping up out of the bushes."

He didn't respond, so I went on, trying now to soften what I'd said. "Don't pay any attention to me today, Cal. Tell me how you've been."

He shrugged, looking like Billy. "I'm all right."

"Do you read a lot, the way Billy does?" I asked to make conversation.

From Cal's expression, I couldn't tell if he pitied me or hated me. He didn't answer, and when Billy poked him, trying to get him to say something, Cal took off running.

"He thinks you don't like him," Billy said. "I know he's a pain, and I'll try to talk to him."

Then I really felt guilty. For Pete's sake, what difference did it make if Cal acted like a jerk? Billy and I would still be friends.

At least I considered Billy to be my friend. But I knew I was more than that to him.

Now I had two things to feel guilty about, and when we got close to my house, I was relieved. I needed to put some distance between Billy and me, so I didn't ask him to come in. When I said good-bye, I avoided his eyes. One of these days I was going to have to have that conversation with him—the one where I told him that we could be only friends. That would be hard to do.

Dad was home already. He taught at the local college, so

he usually got home in time to watch the news on TV and argue with the commentator. "You're an idiot and a liar!" I heard him yell from the living room, so I knew the commentator was talking about prices again.

Dominic slouched past me in the hall, rolling his eyes and heading for the back door. He knew better than to hang around when Dad was talking back to the television set about money. Dog food was getting expensive.

I was helping Mom with dinner when the doorbell rang. It was our neighbor again.

"Your dog . . ." she began.

"Is dead on the sidewalk," I finished and went out to get Dominic.

Just as I bent down to grab Dominic's collar, I saw something move across the street, behind the van parked there. I didn't get a clear look, and I wondered if it was Cal. But he would have gone home with Billy, because neither of them had any reason to hang around on my street. I turned my attention to my big, fat canine problem.

Dominic didn't want to go in the house, so I had to drag him. The phone rang just as I shut the door behind him, and I ran to answer it.

Zack was calling. "Well, we got a reaction to Trumpet's speech."

Something in Zack's voice warned me that I was about to hear bad news. "What happened?"

"Somebody let the air out of Trumpet's tires."

"So?" I asked.

"Teddy, listen to this. Trumpet saw Billy hanging around the parking lot after school. He thinks Billy did it."

"That's ridiculous! Billy wouldn't do anything like that! He was waiting for me."

"But Trumpet doesn't know that. I think I'll go by Billy's house tonight and warn him."

"Good idea," I said. "I know he didn't do it. And his

brother was with him. Cal could be a witness if Billy needs one."

"You're kidding, I hope. Cal's a little creep, and no one would believe anything he said."

All my guilty feelings boiled over. "He's not so bad," I insisted. "He's been lonely since his mother died, that's all."

"My little sister's in his class," Zack said. "She told me he's always in trouble. Maybe *he* let the air out of Trumpet's tires."

"Why would he do that? Trumpet's not his principal, and he doesn't even know about the Student Justice Committee."

"By the time the guilty guy gets caught, Billy will be blamed for everything. Maybe I ought to have a talk with him. You know, tell him that he should quit cutting classes and wandering around like a loose wheel. We used to be able to talk about anything when we were kids, remember? Maybe he'll listen to me now."

I couldn't help but be impressed with how much Zack cared about Billy. I guess he and I were the only ones who really did. To everybody else, Billy was a sort of shadow.

After Zack hung up, I went back to the kitchen. Mom was taking chicken out of the oven, and it looked funny but smelled wonderful. My mouth watered.

"Are you all right?" Mom asked.

"I'm hungry," I told her.

"Was that Mrs. Dimwitly at the door?"

I'd already forgotten Dominic's escape trick. "Yes. Dominic got out again."

Mom shook her head. "How does he do it? Are you sure he's not jumping over the fence?"

"Never. Not unless the cow really jumps over the moon."

After dinner I tried to do my homework, but both Lucie and Jo-Sue called to tell me that Billy had let the air out of

Trumpet's tires. I defended Billy because I was sure he hadn't done it. No way.

I had a hard time falling asleep that night, and when I did I had nightmares.

I dreamed that Devon was taking me to the prom. Just as we were getting ready to leave, Zack came running in, yelling that Billy needed us and we had to go to him quickly. I asked Zack again and again what was wrong, but he kept yelling that we had to hurry. Then somehow we were little kids again and Billy fell off the roof of Bart Pearson's old barn—just as he did in real life. Zack and I loaded him into Zack's old red wagon and hauled him all the way home.

And over our heads, the great cosmic bad-luck machine was rumbling.

Chapter Seven

AT SCHOOL THE next day I heard that Billy spent almost an hour in Trumpet's office. I caught up with Billy in the hall between second and third periods to ask him what had happened.

"Nothing much." He smiled easily at me. "Don't worry."

"That's it? You're just going to tell me not to worry?"

He shrugged. "Hey, I talked to Cal. He won't hang around when we're walking home anymore."

I blinked. Billy could change the subject better than anyone else. "Thanks" was all I had a chance to say before Billy drifted away as if he didn't have a trouble in the world.

But the *Gazette* staff had troubles. We did our best to turn out a good first issue, but with half the staff gone, the best thing that could be said about the paper was that it was boring. We worried ourselves sick.

The *Gazette* came out on Friday, and by noon a dozen students asked me what happened. The athletes liked the sports page, which hadn't changed much, but the rest of the paper was just what I predicted it would be: a bird-cage liner. We were embarrassed.

Trumpet was delighted with it, though, and dragged me out of my chemistry class to congratulate himself on the article about the Student Justice Committee. His only complaint was about the gossip column, which I had written in haste while eating a large cinnamon roll in the back of the cafeteria. He said it need to be "jazzed up."

"What do you mean, 'jazzed up'?" I asked.

He waved his copy of the *Gazette*. "It's not as *perky* as the ones in last year's papers. You wrote that one student spent a weekend helping out at a wildlife preserve and that another student won an audition for a Christmas ballet. Who cares about things like that?"

What did he expect? I thought glumly. The gossip column never interested me and still didn't.

"Now *this* is what I mean." Trumpet waved another piece of paper. "I've done a sample column for you so that you can see how it should be done."

He waited while I read the sample column, and he jittered up and down like a nervous crane. I had a hard time concentrating.

"You see?" he said when I finished. "That's what a real gossip column is like. I should know, because I wrote one for *my* high school paper. Do you get the hang of it now?"

All I could do was nod. I was still nodding when I left his office. The sample column was full of silly stuff like, "Guess who's getting a new car for graduation?" and "Which basketball player is planning to take the head cheerleader to the Christmas dance?" I knew that many high school papers had columns like that, but the *Gazette* had always been different. We won prizes all the time, and most of our general editors went on to work for college papers. The *Gazette* was special.

At lunch I asked Lucie how I was supposed to find idiotic fluff for the gossip column. I couldn't see myself standing out in the hall with a notebook asking kids as they walked past to tell me who they went out with and how much their cars cost.

"Don't worry about it," she told me. "We'll tell everyone that you want social items for the *Gazette*. You'll be up to your ears in news flashes."

She was right. By three o'clock that afternoon, I had a boxful of little scraps of paper, big sheets of paper, and even one four-page life story. I took the box with me when we went to the movie and read some of the items aloud to the staff while we were on our way in Zack's station wagon.

"Here we go, group," I announced, unfolding one hastily written bit of news. "This is from Tess, who wants the world to know that her braces come off in two weeks and that she has a date for the Halloween dance. With a junior-varsity basketball player."

There was a brief silence in the station wagon, and then everyone laughed. "Is there a connection between her braces, Halloween, and the JV player?" Devon asked soberly.

I looked up at him and saw that he was grinning.

"If there *is* a connection, I don't want to know what it is," Zack said. "Read on, MacDuff."

I unfolded another scrap of paper. "Guess who forgot her activity card and couldn't get into the game last weekend?"

"Who cares?" Zack shouted. "What does that piece of paper say?"

"That's what it says. 'Guess who forgot her activity card and couldn't get into the game?'"

I pulled out slips of paper by the handful and gave some of the big newsbreaks to everyone but Zack, who was driving. We took turns reading them aloud, and we hadn't gone one mile before the terrible truth was revealed.

"The people who turned stuff in are the people who are boring," Fine said. I'd never heard her say so much at one time. Every word was a jewel.

"And each one of them wrote several items," Sure added.

"Never have so few written so much garbage," Zack

44

said. "What are you going to do, Teddy? You can't use that stuff. It's horrible."

"Trumpet would love it." I pawed through the box hopelessly.

"But everyone else will hate it. You'll have to edit the best ones and see if you can get enough for a column."

"It would be easier to do the whole thing myself. I'll use these for ideas, and see if I can get more information from some of the people."

"That sounds like a lot of work." Devon was sitting next to Lucie, and he handed back his share of the gossip items. I grabbed to catch them before they fell, and our hands touched for a moment. "I'd help if I could, but I've got all I can handle right now. Besides, I don't have your sense of humor."

"Nobody has Teddy's sense of humor," Fine said loyally. I could have kissed her.

"I need it," I told them. "It takes all the humor I've got to keep from banging my head against the wall right outside Trumpet's office."

"He'd turn you in to the Justice Committee for littering the hall with your blood," Devon said, and everyone laughed.

Devon fit right in. I hadn't realized it until then, but he was perfectly suited for work on the *Gazette*. He had the same wacky sense of humor the rest of us had. I settled down comfortably in the car, prepared to enjoy the afternoon. Maybe this wasn't a real date with Devon, but it was close enough for now.

After the movie, we all went out to dinner together, and while we were waiting to be served, I drew caricatures of all of us on paper napkins. Devon insisted that I sign his, so I wrote "Teddy Gideon" in my very best calligraphy across the corner of the napkin, next to my personal teddy-bear symbol. I was tempted to add my phone number, but that would have been a little obvious. If he wanted my number, he wouldn't have any trouble getting it.

That afternoon was wonderful. I had the best time I'd had for a while, but I was home by seven-thirty and in bed by ten.

In spite of my resolve to stay awake and think about Devon, I fell asleep almost instantly, but Dominic, who slept in my bedroom, woke me up a few minutes later. He was standing by my window, looking out and whining.

I got up and went to the window, wondering what the big old idiot had seen that caused him to act so sad. Across the street, under the streetlight, Billy stood alone. He was looking at our porch, as though I might come out any minute. He had the collar of his jacket turned up against the night chill, and his hands were in his pockets. The way his shoulders were hunched told me that he was unhappy. And lonely.

A few years before, when Billy and I were younger, I would have opened my window and called to him. Then I would have invited him in for hot chocolate, and we would have played Monopoly. But we were too old for hot chocolate and Monopoly now, and I could never feel romantic about him. The awful truth was that Billy never really needed anybody but Billy—and a lot of silence. Me? I needed all my pals and laughter and talk and, yes, even a squabble once in a while, just to keep me on my toes.

Billy walked away, all alone in the dark. Dominic went back to the rug beside my bed and flopped down with a thump that rocked the house. I watched Billy until he was out of sight, and I wondered how many times he had stood outside my house, watching a door that wasn't going to open.

Weekends are quiet in my house. Mom works on Saturdays, teaching English classes for foreign students. Dad putters around the yard, filling in the holes that Dominic digs. If it's raining, he reads. So after I finish my chores, I have the day to myself. That Saturday I went to the hospital with Lucie to visit Miss Bilky.

Miss Bilky was wearing a cast on her leg that went from her toes to her hip, and she wasn't very happy about it. This was the first time I ever saw her looking anything but perfect. Her hair, which was that nice iron-gray color, was as rumpled as Dominic's, and without makeup, she looked like a different person.

"How are you feeling?" I asked her.

"How do I look like I'm feeling?" she grumbled. Her bed was piled with books. Even in the hospital, she was still working.

"You look tired," Lucie said tactfully. "I hope you aren't in any pain."

Miss Bilky made a gesture that said she didn't care about that. "I still can't believe I fell off that ladder. I've changed that porch light a dozen times without any problems."

"You were lucky that your neighbor saw you," Lucie said.

"My luck ran out." Miss Bilky shoved her books aside. "Mr. Trumpteller was here this morning."

Lucie and I sat down next to her bed. "Oh," we said in unison.

"Yes, indeed." Miss Bilky looked thoughtful. "He doesn't feel that he has your full cooperation in certain areas. He has a sentimental interest in the paper—he mentioned that he'd worked on one himself a long time ago. I'd suggest that you show him a little more tact and patience."

Lucie and I exchanged glances. "We'll try," we said, but I thought she was expecting an awful lot of us.

Miss Bilky leaned her head against her pillow and sighed. She looked more than tired. I knew she wasn't a young woman, but now she actually looked old. If she'd been feeling better I would have told her exactly what I thought about the Student Justice Committee and how hard things were for us since Steve and his staff quit. But I couldn't worry her now.

Lucie leaned forward. "You get well," she told Miss Bilky. "Until then, we'll muddle along."

Good old Lucie. She knew exactly how to put things, even if she stretched the truth a little. To call what we were doing "muddling" was being charitable.

Our hospital visit was a short one, but we promised that we'd be back soon. Lucie had an appointment with her doctor for another allergy shot then. Our problems on the *Gazette* were making her sick because she had most of the responsibility. I didn't envy her.

"I'm using about a case of tissues a day now," she told me disgustedly. "My nose is so red and shiny that yesterday Bobo Bitterman held his hands over his eyes and told everyone I was blinding him."

We were walking down the street from the hospital to the clinic and a cold wind was blowing, promising rain by nightfall. "Bobo Bitterman would be lucky if the only thing wrong with him was the color of *his* nose," I said scornfully. "He's just mad because Zack points out all his fumbles on the sports page, sometimes in headlines."

"He's going to get a football scholarship," Lucie said, blowing her nose angrily.

"That's the only way he can get into college," I told her. "His IQ is smaller than his shoe size."

"His ego's big enough. Look, I'll probably have to wait a long time for my shot. Why don't you go on home?"

I made up my mind in a hurry, since sitting in a doctor's waiting room is not very high on my list of great ways to spend a Saturday afternoon. "I'll drop by Jo-Sue's," I told her. "She might need some moral support, since we're starting the demerit system on Monday."

Lucie stopped in the clinic doorway. "You're right. And

48

the Student Justice Committee meets for the first time next Friday. Give her my sympathy. If I finish up here before dinnertime, I'll come by and the three of us can scream together."

We waved good-bye, and I caught the bus to Jo-Sue's. She was always home on Saturday afternoons, baby-sitting her little sisters while her mother shopped. But today her mother met me at the door and told me that Jo-Sue had driven to Riverford to visit her married sister. I knew then that Jo-Sue was really upset. Any time she went to Kathy's, it was because she needed advice.

I went for a long walk. I love walking alone, especially in autumn when the leaves first begin to fall. I thought about Billy, standing alone outside my house the night before, and I wondered how I was going to tell him that I wanted us to be only friends.

I also thought about Devon, who seemed to grow more attractive each day. I loved the way he laughed. I loved the way he looked. I even loved that elusive quality about him when I wasn't hating it. Without a doubt, he was different from any of the boys I had ever known. Of course, I'd known them from their romper and sandbox days, and we had no secrets from each other. Catherwood is too small for that. But Devon seemed to hold back from letting anyone get to know him too well too fast. It was frustrating but fascinating.

For instance, I seldom saw him walking in the halls at school with the same person twice. Of course, he was new at school, and it takes time to make friends. But sometimes I got the impression that Devon was in no hurry to get in with any special group—not even the other athletes.

But he was fitting in with the rest of the *Gazette* staff. Miss Bilky was going to appreciate his humor. He was a good writer too, and he had a real sense of what was news. Lucie had told me that she didn't do much editing on

Devon's work because it didn't need it. I was proud for him.

I was smiling when I walked through my front door an hour later. Dad gave me a message from Zack, who wanted me to call him immediately, if not sooner.

I had to call three times before I got through to him, and then the first thing he did was complain.

"Where is everybody? I can't reach Lucie, and Sure went to the dentist. Where have *you* been?"

"Out," I said. "What do you want?"

"Devon and Fine and I thought it might be fun if we all got together again tonight. We could go out for pizza or whatever. What do you think?"

"Is everybody going?"

"Well, how do I know?" Zack said. "I haven't been able to reach the others. Devon and Fine are going, and I sure want to. I'm bored right out of my skull."

Devon and Fine? What did he mean, "Devon and Fine are going," anyway? I almost asked him, but I stopped myself just in time. They wouldn't be out on a real date. This was only another get-together of the *Gazette* staff. We had them all the time.

"Well?"

"Sure," I said, trying to seem cheerful. "That sounds good to me. Lucie should be home pretty soon."

"I'll call you back when I've got everything set up." Zack hung up before I could ask him what time he had in mind.

Dad was standing right behind me when I hung up. "Going out?"

"Just for a pizza with the *Gazette* kids."

He pulled one earlobe, a signal that he was about to ask me to do something that I definitely would not want to do. "Why don't you invite Billy to go along? He used to hang around here all the time, and the two of you and Zack did everything together."

"Billy used to hang around our *family,*" I said. "And he wouldn't come tonight even if I asked him, because all the kids who are going work on the *Gazette.* Billy never does anything that's connected with school. He doesn't even show up for classes half the time."

"He's a very smart young man," Dad said defensively.

I sighed. "It doesn't have anything to do with being smart or dumb. It has to do with being involved."

"My daughter, the psychologist," Dad said. "Did it ever occur to you that maybe Billy has a hard time getting involved? His life is pretty hard, what with his mother being dead and his father . . ."

I supplied the words Dad didn't want to use. "Not caring?"

Dad looked away and let go of his earlobe. "I wouldn't put it that way."

"No, but I would, because it's the truth. Billy's dad doesn't care about anything but himself. He doesn't even care about Cal."

"When you're older . . ."

"No," I said, "I won't understand it then either. Just because your wife dies, you don't need to forget about your children."

I went up to my room then, with Dominic right behind me. I wasn't mad at Dad, but I wasn't going to make any excuses for Mr. McGill either. When things need to be done, we have to do them, right? That's how life is. You'd think Billy's dad could figure that out.

But I didn't want to think about Billy. I'd be seeing Devon soon, and I wanted to think about that. I took a quick shower and wrapped up in my fuzzy old robe while I pawed through my closet, looking for the absolutely perfect outfit. For once I didn't spend a lot of time regretting the size of my feet.

Maybe Devon was slow in picking special friends, but when he got around to picking a special girl, I wanted very much to be her.

51

Chapter Eight

ZACK PICKED UP Lucie and Sure before he stopped at my house, and I felt a small pang when he told me that Devon had picked up Fine to save time. I hoped that saving time was the only reason, and I kept telling myself that this was only a casual get-together of the *Gazette* staff.

We met at the pizza place just north of town. Devon and Fine were already there, and they had saved a big table in the back for us. The place was already crowded and noisy, which suited us perfectly. We needed a lot of racket to cheer ourselves up.

Zack gave our orders to the waiter and was about to launch into one of his long tales about life in the team locker room when Lucie interrupted him.

"There's something we ought to be talking about, guys." She banged on the table with her fist. "This meeting is now called to order. We're going to discuss adding people to the general news staff. Devon can't handle it all himself, and I'm too busy to be of any real help. Any suggestions?"

"Get somebody from the journalism class." Zack was fishing ice out of his water glass and crunching it between his big white teeth.

"Idiot," I said. "We *are* the journalism class."

"No, I mean the first-semester kids."

"Miss Bilky doesn't let freshmen work on the paper," Lucie pointed out.

"She let Teddy do cartoons when *she* was only a freshman," Zack said through a mouthful of ice.

"That was different," Lucie said. "Teddy didn't write for the paper until she was a sophomore." She took Zack's water glass away from him. "Honestly, Zack, if you don't stop acting like a slob, we're going to make you eat in the back room."

"We've been thinking," the twins said in unison.

"No thinking until you're juniors," Zack told them, reaching for my water glass. I slapped his hand and moved my glass. He could make me laugh even when I didn't want to.

Lucie smiled at the twins. "What were you thinking about?"

"Maybe one of us could help with general news, for a while at least," Fine said shyly, looking at Devon. Her clear, pretty skin flushed pink.

The idea made sense, because both of the girls at least had a little experience, but my stomach twisted into a knot. My plans for Devon didn't include his working with Fine.

Devon spoke up then. "We could try it." He seemed a little too pleased.

"Why not?" Lucie said. "For a few weeks, anyway. But no promises about it being permanent, okay?"

"Fine," said Fine. She and Sure giggled.

The pizzas came, but I could only poke at mine. My imagination was rolling along at top speed, convincing me that before very long, Fine and Devon would be going steady and I'd find myself at the prom with Zack, who would no doubt show up wearing bunny slippers and a shower cap. He does things like that.

We ended up having a serious discussion over our ice cream about the Student Justice Committee, and everyone agreed that Billy was going to be in for a hard time. While the others were talking about Trumpet's various personality problems, Devon leaned close to me and said, "Billy's a good friend of yours, isn't he?"

"Just for my whole life," I said. Then I realized how that might sound. "What I mean is, we've known each other since we were little kids."

But even while I said it, I remembered how I felt when I saw Billy standing outside in the dark, looking at my house. I didn't think "friends" was the right word, but I couldn't think of any other. Oh, darn, why had they brought up Billy tonight? I thought. I felt so guilty that I couldn't even stand to think about him.

Sure had been complaining all evening about having a headache, something that always happens to her when she goes to the dentist, and Fine worries about her just as if they were real sisters, so they decided they wanted to go home. They really were sweet girls, even though I was jealous of Fine, so I was actually sorry when Sure called her dad to come get her, and Fine went along to keep her company.

The rest of us had another round of soft drinks and gossiped for half an hour. Then Zack, who has a great career ahead of him starting riots and wars, said, "It's time for me to take Teddy away from all this. She's madly in love with me and wants me to take her to Last Mile Point for a serious discussion."

"Dream on, fool," I grouched. "I'm not going to Last Mile Point with anybody, and I wouldn't be caught dead there with someone who stores his dirty gym clothes and old apple cores in his car."

Lucie drank the last of her pop and stood up. "Let's be efficient about this. Zack and I live practically next door to each other, so he can take me home. And you two live close to school, so Devon can take you home, Teddy."

I worked hard to keep the grin off my face. "That sounds all right with me."

"Then let's go," Devon said, and the four of us left the pizza place together.

Lucie and Zack turned down the street, and Devon led me around to the side of the restaurant, where he had parked. He took my hand to guide me along in the dark. I couldn't think of a single word to say.

Devon did most of the talking on the way home. He told me that his family had moved to Catherwood just before school started, so that his dad could be closer to his job. His sister was in college and worked part-time for the theater that was showing the movie we'd seen. That was how she got us passes.

"She gets them for me every month or so. Next time there's a good movie showing, we can all go again."

"That sounds great. I love movies." I guess I was hinting that I might be available even if the rest of the *Gazette* staff wasn't, but either my hint wasn't strong enough or Devon wasn't interested, because he didn't respond.

When we got to my house, Devon walked to the front door with me. "This was fun. Do you guys go out together very often?"

"Not on any regular basis. Just whenever the mood strikes us." I waited then, unable to think of anything else to say, and Devon waited, too.

It was embarrassing. We just stood there, looking at the front door as if it would open by itself. Then I heard a big "Woof!" from Dominic, who must have finally decided that there really was someone outside.

"You've got a dog?" Devon asked. "It sounds big."

"Would you like to come in for a while and meet the dog? And my folks?" I added hastily. I didn't want him to think that there was something wrong with my parents and that I never let anyone see them.

He hesitated. "Well, only for a few minutes. They probably weren't expecting anyone to drop in on them this late."

I opened the door before he could talk himself out of it,

and there was Dominic, lying on his back in the hall, wagging his tail weakly.

Devon looked down at the mountain of fur and fat. "Is he all right?"

I poked Dominic with my shoe. "Get up!"

Dominic groaned and struggled to his feet. Devon started to laugh.

"That is the goofiest animal I ever saw." Devon patted Dominic's broad head. "What kind is he?"

"He won't tell, and we can't guess. Whenever Dad fills out his dog license applications, he puts 'big' in the space where you're supposed to fill in the breed."

I took Devon into the living room, where my folks were watching TV, and introduced him. Everyone seemed pleased with everyone else, but no one could come up with any brilliant conversation, so Devon and I, with Dominic close behind, wandered off to the kitchen. Without even thinking, I fixed hot chocolate, and we were drinking our second cups before I remembered that Billy and I used to sit there, drinking hot chocolate, on winter Saturday afternoons when we were kids.

Billy again. Somehow I had to find a way of telling him that he wanted more from our relationship than I could give. To be Billy's girl, I'd have to give up being *me*, and I didn't want to be a solitary dreamer like him. I must have had a strange expression on my face, because Devon asked, "Is something wrong?"

I looked up at him, at those dark eyes under straight black eyebrows, and my ears started ringing again. Suddenly, he leaned forward and touched the end of my nose. "You're awfully cute," he whispered. Then he pulled back, as if he'd done something wrong.

A long, painful silence followed. I was sure something should come after a comment like that, but what? Finally, I babbled, "Thanks, but my feet are too big." Clearly, the great cosmic bad-luck machine was now writing my lines for me.

It was no surprise to me that the next thing Devon said was, "I guess I'd better get going."

I followed him back to the living room, where he said good night to my folks, and then to the door, where he said good night to me.

"Come again," I said miserably. Then I added, with as much sincerity as I could scrape up, "Really. I mean it."

He just nodded, and then he was gone. I held onto the doorknob for a moment after I shut the door. The hall was dimly lighted, and I felt strange and light-headed. And suddenly lonely.

I wanted to run outside and call him back. I wanted to shout, "Wait! I hardly know you!" I wanted to tell him things about myself that I'd never told anyone for fear of being laughed at. I wanted to tell him that I really, really liked him and wasn't always such an idiot.

But I went upstairs to get ready for bed.

I had been in bed for half an hour, restless and miserable, and not just because of my brilliant conversation in the kitchen. When I couldn't stand it any longer, I got up and looked out the window.

Billy wasn't there. The street stretched away empty and lonely, and a few leaves blew along the sidewalk under the streetlight where he had stood the other night. Relieved, I crawled back into bed.

Chapter Nine

ON MONDAY THE demerit system started. I'd forgotten all about it, so guess who collected a demerit slip from a hall monitor for being late to first period?

I hadn't had much chance to talk to Jo-Sue over the weekend—just one brief phone call on Sunday—so we had a lot to catch up on during lunch.

"My sister thinks the Student Justice Committee might be a good thing," she told Lucie and me.

"You're kidding," I said. "I always thought Kathy was smart."

Jo-Sue bit neatly into her sandwich. "Of course she's smart, but that doesn't mean I agree with her. It's not that a justice committee is a bad idea, exactly. It's just dumb, if you see what I mean. Anyway, she told me I ought to give it a try for the time being and not do anything extreme."

"What do you mean, 'extreme'?" Lucie asked.

"She means that she isn't going to resign as junior-class president or punch out Trumpet's lights," I offered. My sandwich wasn't as good as Jo-Sue's—she had bacon and tomato. In a moment of complete madness that morning, I actually remembered to take the lunch Mom fixed for me. Tuna fish and sprouts on what looked like the sole of one of Dad's gardening shoes.

"Kathy says that the kids here get away with murder. And we know that's true," Jo-Sue said. "What Trumpet expects from us is responsible behavior. Or anyway, that's what Kathy said."

"She's a traitor." I rolled up the tuna fish, sprouts, and old boot in a napkin and tossed them in the trash can. "I love Kathy, but I think getting married dried up her brain or something."

Jo-Sue sighed. "I was hoping you'd say that she has a point and sort of encourage me."

"You don't sound convinced yourself," Lucie said.

"I'm not, but I agreed to wait for a while and see what happens."

"So look over there and see what's happening," I told Jo-Sue, and I pointed across the cafeteria, where a hall monitor was writing out a demerit slip for a poor, scared freshman who had thrown a paper cup toward the trash can near the door and missed.

"So next time he'll try harder," Lucie said. "You have to admit, Teddy, that this place looks like a pigpen when we get through with it."

"Hey!" I cried. "Get off my case, will you? I'm only saying what everyone else is saying. Since when are you knocking yourself out to get in good with Trumpet?"

That wasn't fair, and I knew it. But when we got up to leave, I noticed that the floor was a lot cleaner than usual. Of course, there were three monitors watching, with their pencils and little pads ready—and smirks on their faces.

By last period, some of the kids were comparing their collections of demerits, but others weren't laughing. I was beginning to feel uneasy, the way I do when the big old cosmic bad-luck machine is coming my way.

When I got to the *Gazette* office after school, Devon and Fine were already there, whispering in the corner. They looked up just as I walked in, and I had a hunch I interrupted something.

"So what's new?" I said, more to make conversation

than anything else. I was working hard at pretending that I didn't care.

"Devon asked me to interview the cheerleaders about their trip to Seattle," Fine told me.

"She got some good notes," he said. "She'll be great at this job."

Fine was blushing again. She and Devon moved to the table and sat down next to each other. They looked cute together. I dropped my books at the other end of the table and pretended to look for something in one of my folders.

This is none of your business, I told myself. They're just working together.

But Fine kept looking up at Devon from under her lashes, and I was having a hard time remembering that he had told me I was cute that night in my kitchen. Not that it meant anything, but I wanted it to.

Lucie and Zack came in together. Zack had three demerit slips in one hand and a bag of potato chips in the other.

"They won't let me eat in the hall!" he complained. "I got three of these lousy slips between the vending machine in the cafeteria and here."

"Life is one endless tragedy," Lucie said sourly. Her nose was red again, so I guess her allergy shots weren't working very well. I was shocked to see the edge of a demerit slip sticking out from one of her books. Next to Jo-Sue, Lucie is the most perfect girl around. What was happening to us?

Lucie sat down at her desk and twirled her chair around to face us. "Does anyone have any big bulletins to pass along?"

Zack crunched his potato chips. "Everything is okay in my department."

Sure came in then, looking as if she'd been crying. I'd never seen her so upset. She slammed her books down on

60

the table and pulled a couple of those dumb pink slips from her pocket. "Look at this! I got two of them today."

"From the hall monitors?" I asked.

"No. One was from the custodian, because I left my locker door open. The other was from one of the cooks. I left my tray on the table at lunch." All that talking must have exhausted her, because she slumped in her chair, blushing just like Fine.

"Cheer up," Zack told her. "You'll survive this. Tomorrow will be a brighter day. March on."

"Sure," said Sure. "Why don't you just shut up, Zack?"

We sat and brooded for a few minutes, and then the twins took off with Zack. Lucie was busy reviewing some odds and ends on her desk, and Devon was writing his lead story, so I got out my sketch pad and tried to come up with a cartoon idea for the next edition.

I'd been trying all day, whenever I got a spare minute to think, and so far I'd come up with exactly nothing. Now I racked my brain, doodled on the page, and finally gave up.

There was still plenty of time, but I never liked leaving the cartoon until the last minute. Or even the last few days.

"Are you done?" Lucie asked me.

"I haven't even started."

She gathered up her stuff. "Don't worry about it. Are you leaving now?"

I glanced at Devon, wondering if he was going to stay much longer. He looked up, as if he knew I was thinking about him, and smiled.

"I guess I might as well leave," I said to Lucie. "I'm not getting any ideas."

"I'll walk with you," Devon said.

Lucie grinned at me as we left. She must have realized how pleased I was.

Devon and I were halfway across the parking lot when I remembered Billy.

He nearly always waited for me after school those days,

but this time I didn't see him anywhere, and I was glad. I hadn't given any thought about how I would handle the situation if I came out with Devon and Billy was there. That would be a disaster, I decided. Thinking about it made me so uncomfortable that I didn't enjoy my walk with Devon as much as I might have if the Billy problem had been solved.

Devon didn't walk all the way home with me—he only went as far as the intersection and then turned off to his street. And he didn't say much of anything—just small talk. I don't know what I expected. Something, anything, that would assure me that he wasn't too interested in Fine.

When I got home, I found that Mom was out somewhere, shopping probably, so I went up to my room to change clothes and glare at my demerit slips. Catherwood High was turning into a jail, I decided.

I turned on my stereo and lay down on my bed. There was no point in thinking about demerits anymore. And there wasn't much point in thinking about Devon either, although it was hard not to. I was uncomfortably aware of the discouraging possibility that he was on my mind a lot more than I was on his. Just about the time I thought he was beginning to be interested in me, he started showing more than a business interest in Fine. Then he walked partway home with me. Partway, and he said nothing that I'd want to bother writing about in my diary. Not that I keep one, but if I did, that day's conversation wouldn't have been worth recording. So where does that leave me? I thought.

Spending my time trying to think up an idea for my next cartoon.

Impossible! I got off my bed and went downstairs to get a soft drink from the refrigerator. The kitchen door opened then and Mom came in. She was carrying a sack of groceries, which she handed to me. "Here. Make yourself useful to your poor old mother."

"Sure, Poor Old Mother." I followed her out to the kitchen with the sack.

"I just saw the oddest thing," she said. "Billy's little brother was trying to hide behind the bushes across the street. When I called out to him, he started running almost as if he'd been up to something he was ashamed of."

Cal was probably planning to be a spy when he grew up. "He's just impossible. Don't pay any attention to him."

I was unpacking the bag of groceries when it occurred to me that if Mom saw Cal, Billy was probably around somewhere. "You didn't see Billy, did you?" I asked Mom. I was remembering the night he'd stood across the street, watching the house, and I wondered if he'd been doing it again.

"No, Billy wasn't around. Why?"

"No reason." I didn't want Mom and Dad to find out that Billy had been out there in the dark all alone, looking miserable. They'd think up a quick solution, and I could just hear them telling me to pay more attention to Billy so he wouldn't be so lonesome.

But it bothered me. Could Billy have been out there somewhere, and Mom just didn't see him? Why would Cal be standing in front of our house? He sure didn't like me.

I suddenly wondered if maybe Cal was lonely for a family. He hadn't been very old when his mother died, and he probably didn't remember the times when she brought him to visit Mom. He'd been just a baby then. But maybe Billy told him. Maybe Cal wanted to be close to us because we'd been close to his mother.

But maybe he was just hanging around to bug me. That sounded more like Cal.

When I went to bed that night, I looked out the window again. No one was there. More leaves had fallen, and a light rain glittered in the glow from the streetlight. The scene made me feel so lonely that I shivered.

63

Chapter Ten

THE STUDENT JUSTICE Committee met on Friday during first period. Devon covered it for the *Gazette,* and I gnawed on my fingernails all through my first class, wondering how Jo-Sue was handling the situation. In spite of my original objection to being involved, even as a reporter, I ended up wanting to go. But only the general news editor was invited. When I asked Trumpet if I could look on to get an idea for a cartoon, he gave me a look that aged me ten years. No answer, just a look. It was enough.

I didn't see Jo-Sue until lunch, when she joined Lucie and me halfway through dessert.

"Where have you been?" I croaked through a mouthful of dry chocolate cake, the day's special dessert. "We've been worrying about you."

"You weren't so worried that you lost your appetite," Jo-Sue snarled as she sat down.

She had stopped by the counter and loaded up a tray, so Lucie and I had to wait while she munched her way through a sandwich, scowling the whole time. Her hair was pulled into little peaks again.

"Okay," Lucie said when Jo-Sue had taken the edge off her hunger. "What happened at the meeting?"

"It was awful. And *dumb.* We were so embarrassed."

"That doesn't tell us anything," I groaned. "Who did what and why?"

Jo-Sue fixed me with a desperate look. "If you're wondering about Billy, yes, his name came up. And he got thirty hours in the penalty study hall."

Lucie sucked in her breath. For a moment I was so angry that I thought I was going to scream.

"I hope you're kidding," I said to Jo-Sue. "I'm too young to have a stroke."

She shook her head, unable to answer because her mouth was full of that awful stale cake. While she was swallowing, she took a piece of paper from her purse and handed it to me.

It was another set of Trumpet's guidelines, this time for the student judges. I was beginning to believe that the man never slept. He probably sat up every night thinking up new rules and regulations.

There was a long list of "crimes" on the page, and each of them had a number after it. "Do these numbers mean demerits?" I asked.

"Yes," Jo-Sue answered, having finished her cake at last. "Once you accumulate ten demerits, you have to appear before the committee. Then we decide if your big fat criminal behavior is bad enough for the demerits to be changed into hours in penalty study hall."

I handed the paper back to her. "How did Billy get thirty demerits?"

"Late to class. In the halls without a pass. Skipping class. Leaving class without permission. Leaving school in the middle of the day. You name it and he did it. Actually, he had nearly forty demerits, but we cut them back to thirty." Jo-Sue tasted her milk and made a face. "This isn't cow's milk. It must be from a yak."

"No, actually it's armadillo milk," Lucie said. "For Pete's sake, drink it or don't drink it, but keep talking. What else happened?"

"I'm not done talking about Billy yet," Jo-Sue complained. "Don't rush me. What made everything worse was that he didn't even show up."

Good for you, Billy, I thought. "What did Trumpet do?"

"He gave Billy ten demerits for that, to be used against him next time."

I slumped against the table and groaned. "At this rate, Billy will be in penalty study hall until he's ready for his old-age pension."

"At least," Jo-Sue said.

"Did anyone show up?" Lucie asked.

"Sure," Jo-Sue replied. "Half a dozen scared freshmen and Bobo—who laughed through the whole thing—and one of the cheerleaders, who said that her rights were being violated. She wanted a lawyer. Trumpet took her out of the meeting, so I don't know what happened."

"Hmm," Lucie mused. "Who was it?"

"Bonnie."

Lucie began laughing. "Her dad's a lawyer. No wonder Mr. Trumpteller took her out of the meeting. This may be the last we hear of the Student Justice Committee."

That cheered us up, and we were smiling when we left the cafeteria. But Lucie was wrong. Whatever Bonnie may have said to Trumpet or her father, the demerit system stayed. Each morning the penalty study hall was open for business. But Billy never showed.

After school that day, I dropped by the *Gazette* office to sort through the rest of the gossip items, which had been trickling in ever since we spread the word. The column was nearly finished, but I still didn't have an idea for the cartoon.

Fine and Devon were whispering in the corner again. I tried to pretend I didn't see them and sat down next to Zack. He was full of news about how people reacted to the Justice Committee, and he was dangerously close to appearing before it himself—he had six demerits by then.

"Let's go somewhere tonight," he proposed. "We all need to get our minds off our troubles."

"Sounds good to me," I said, but Lucie shook her head.

"Not me. I've got a paper due on Monday."

Sure had come in while we were talking, and she wasn't interested in going out either. Fine and Devon didn't hear Zack at first, and after he repeated himself, both of them shook their heads, too.

My heart sank to my stomach. I was absolutely sure they had a date, and I didn't want to hear about it. Don't ask me how I knew. I guess there was something about the way they looked at each other. I'd been hoping that Devon might want to see me that weekend, or even the next. There was a school dance coming up too, and I didn't have a date. The possibilities were endless, but the certainty seemed to be that I wasn't going anywhere with Devon except in my imagination.

The whole thing was so depressing that I bundled up my gossip items and my books and left. Zack was the only one who said good-bye.

I hadn't seen Billy all day, and I was worried about him, so I hoped that he would be hanging around the parking lot. But he wasn't, so I walked home alone.

The minute I got in the door, I called Jo-Sue, hoping that she'd want to get together for the evening, but she had a last-minute date with the senior she'd been going out with on and off for two years. She wasn't crazy about him, but seeing him was better than staying home.

"I can't concentrate on anything," she said. "I feel as if people are giving me dirty looks. Or avoiding me."

"You've got a date tonight," I reminded her. "At least someone isn't avoiding you."

"Oh, him," she scoffed. "We're taking his little sister and two of her friends to the movie with us."

"Fun," I groaned.

"More fun than tomorrow night. No one asked me to the dance, so if I go, I have to go alone."

"It's no big deal," I said, reassuring myself. "No live music. I didn't want to go all that much, anyway."

"We could go together," she suggested.

"And stand around all night waiting for someone to ask us to dance? We did that last year."

Jo-Sue sighed. "How come I'm junior-class president and I don't have a date for the first dance of the year?"

"Only one of the cheerleaders has a real date for tomorrow," I told her. "And that's because she's going steady."

"You're joking," she protested. "No, I believe you. What's wrong with everybody this year?"

"Need you ask?" I said. "It's Trumpet. He's like a blight on the school. Nobody has fun anymore. We spend all our time wondering if a hall monitor is going to pop out of the woodwork and hand us a demerit for breathing. I'll even bet the monitors will bring their pencils and notebooks to the dance."

"Oh, fun," Jo-Sue said crossly. "But I think you're right. It really is Trumpet. Just seeing him walk down the hall is enough to ruin my day now."

We didn't cheer each other up. By the time we said good-bye, I think both of us were ready to cry.

My folks went out that night, and I was in bed and asleep by ten o'clock.

The next day—Saturday—I went to see Miss Bilky again. She looked much better, and we had a dandy visit. Zack came in just before I left, bringing Miss Bilky an enormous potted plant, a stack of new magazines, and a paperback book with a sexy cover.

She offered Zack one of the chocolates I'd brought her. "You two are spoiling me."

"We're trying to persuade you to leave this dump and come back to school," Zack told her. "We need you. The librarian is trying, but she doesn't know any more about how the *Gazette* works than Trumpet does."

"She's more fun, though," I added.

Miss Bilky looked worried. "Are things that bad?"

"Wait until you get back," Zack said gloomily. "Nothing is the same anymore."

"We'll adjust," I said, giving Zack a warning look. "It's just that it'd be better if we had you around, so take care of yourself and come back as soon as you can." Then I pinched Zack's arm until he yelped and practically dragged him out of the room. "Can't you see how tired she is?" I demanded.

Zack winced. "Yeah, I should have kept my mouth shut."

"Permanently," I said. "She'll get out of here a lot sooner if she isn't worried about us."

Zack offered me a ride home, but I had errands downtown, so we said our good-byes on the street. I got home about an hour later, just as the rain started. I had prepared for another night at home alone by treating myself to a sack of chocolates. To my astonishment, Mom told me that Devon had called and was going to call back.

"He probably wants to know what Fine's favorite flowers are so he can send her a corsage," I said.

"That's right, there's a dance tonight." Mom turned a page of the book she was reading about a monster alligator living in the Los Angeles sewer system. "But I didn't know it was formal."

"It's not," I said.

"So why would Devon give Fine flowers?" Mom mumbled. Her eyes bugged out suddenly. "I didn't know alligators could do *that!*"

I wandered off, leaving her to her entertainment. I would have gone up to my room, but the phone rang just as I passed it.

"I tried calling you before," Devon said as soon as I answered. "Do you have plans for the dance tonight?"

He wants me to drive him and Fine to the dance because he doesn't have a ride, I told myself. That's the only reason

69

he'd call after all that whispering in the corner of the *Gazette* office.

"I'm not going," I said firmly.

"Would you like to go with me? Or are you mad at me? You sound mad."

"I'm not mad." I was numb from the shoulders up. I simply couldn't think. Was he asking me to go to the dance with him? Alone? Without Fine?

"Is everything all right?" he asked. "You sound funny."

"I'm just fine." The moment I said it, I could have bitten off my tongue. I sounded just like Fine.

"Well, do you want to go?"

I swallowed hard. "Sure. I'd love to."

He said he'd pick me up around eight-thirty, and suddenly the whole day looked better. I called Jo-Sue to tell her, but she wasn't home, so I trotted upstairs to decide what to wear. When I passed my mirror, I saw that I was smiling.

Not many of the kids showed up that night. Probably only fifty Catherwood students had arrived by ten o'clock, and it was clear that the dance was a failure. One of the girls on the dance committee was crying in the girls' john, but I couldn't convince her that sometimes small dances are better than large ones. Somehow it didn't seem right that I was so happy when other people were miserable. But I couldn't keep a smile off my face. I was with Devon.

He seemed even better-looking that night than he ever had before, and he was a wonderful dancer. And he danced every danced with me.

We didn't talk much. Neither of us mentioned demerits or the Student Justice Committee, not even when we were sitting with Lucie. It was a lazy, delicious evening, as far as I was concerned. I didn't mind at all that not many people showed up. I wasn't in the mood for a mob.

Once, when Devon and I were dancing a slow dance, he

whispered, "You really are cute tonight. I was afraid that you weren't going to come with me."

"I was surprised when you called, that's all."

"I would have asked you sooner, but I wasn't sure I could get my dad's car. And things got a little complicated."

I was afraid to ask what the complications were. We were together now, and that was all that was important. Some other time, I told myself dreamily, I'll worry about Fine and the whispers in the corner.

We left early and went across town for hamburgers. I'd finally recovered my ability to talk, so I kept Devon laughing. I couldn't get used to the feelings his smile gave me. I got shivers clear down to my feet.

When he brought me home, the lights in my house were out, so I knew my folks had gone to bed. I wanted to ask Devon to come in, but we'd just eaten and I couldn't think of any other excuse. The evening was ending, and I wanted it to go on and on.

We walked up the steps to the porch together, and I put my hand on the doorknob, ready to go inside. When I looked up to say good night, Devon bent his head and kissed me.

He didn't put his arms around me. He just kissed me, quickly and gently. And then, while I was still standing there dumbfounded, he slipped his arms around my shoulders and kissed me again. Only this time he kissed me harder.

"Good night," he murmured, and he turned and went down the steps.

I slipped inside, pressing one hand against my lips. He kissed me!

Chapter Eleven

I SHOULD HAVE been happy the next day, but I wasn't. I took Dominic out for one of our Sunday walks, and I brooded while he shuffled along investigating every crack in the sidewalk. I got light-headed every time I thought about Devon's kissing me, but I wasn't sure why he'd done it. What about Fine?

And what about Billy? I felt guilty every time he popped into my mind. I was angry with myself, the way I always get when I know I'm disappointing someone. But by that time I was pretty sure that Billy was in love with a Teddy who existed more in his imagination than in real life. Billy needed a poet for a girlfriend, not a cartoonist.

Dominic is not an athletic dog, and we hadn't been out more than half an hour before he decided that it was time to go home. I agreed, because I'd seen Cal sneaking along behind us. Even though for a change he was watching Dominic instead of me, he still made me so angry that I wanted to run back, grab him, and give him a good shaking.

Besides, I'd been away from the house long enough. I'd fantasized that Devon would call me that Sunday afternoon, just because he'd kissed me the night before and didn't want to be out of contact with me for too long.

After I got home, I kept busy and tried not to look at the clock more than once every ten minutes. Devon didn't call.

By dinnertime, I'd convinced myself that Devon kissed

every girl he took out, so why should I make such a big deal out of it? After all, it wasn't as if we had any sort of understanding, right? And since I was taking everything in such a what-the-heck way, he was sure to call that evening.

Ha.

He didn't call.

When I got to school the next morning, I passed the open door of the penalty study hall. Half the students in the room were dozing, heads down on their desks. The rest were looking out the window, watching leaves blowing ahead of a hard north wind. So much for studying, I thought. And Billy wasn't there—not that I'd expected him to be.

No one was in the *Gazette* office yet, so I didn't hang around. I wasn't in the mood to talk, anyway. I found a private corner in the cafeteria and consoled myself with a double cinnamon roll.

About five minutes before first bell, Billy found me and sat down next to me.

"You're too late for penalty study hall and too early for first period. How come?" I asked.

He grinned and shrugged. "There's a storm coming up. You want to walk over to the park and watch the leaves come down?"

Only Billy thinks of things like that, and there's nothing I like better than walking through the park in a storm. But first bell was going to ring any minute and cutting classes wasn't my idea of a terrific way to start out the week.

"Oh, Billy," I sighed. "Why can't you shape up? You can't go on like this. Haven't you gotten enough demerits?"

"Demerits," he said softly, grinning again, and he shook his head as if the whole thing were a kid's game and he didn't have time to play. "Come on, I'll walk you to class. Maybe we can go to the park after school."

I wiped frosting off my fingers with a napkin and got

73

up. "I can't today. I've got stuff I absolutely have to do for the *Gazette.*"

"I'll wait," Billy said.

I shook my head stubbornly. Walking in the park with Billy, during a storm, late in the day—that was too romantic. He'd get ideas I'd never be able to change. We weren't little kids anymore, and the things we did together when we were in grade school seemed to have a different meaning now.

We passed Zack and Devon in the hall, and both of them said "hi." I wanted to bang my head against the wall and scream. Life was not fair. The great cosmic bad-luck machine seemed to be working overtime. Devon probably thought I kissed everyone, including Billy.

The storm broke during second period, and one of the big maple trees on the south lawn blew over. I stood at the window and watched, wishing that Billy and I were ten years old again and over in the park watching the leaves and branches fly.

Everybody on the *Gazette* staff was in the office when I got there after my last class. The twins had put together a nice short piece about the big old tree blowing down—it was as old as the school, maybe even older, and had lots of initials carved on it. They were doing a good job helping Devon. I was in such a bad mood that if I could have found a way of criticizing Fine I would have. But she was even helping me out.

Darn, I thought. It's easier to be jealous of someone you can hate.

And I was trying to hate her, believe me. Each time I looked at her, she was looking at Devon, and he kept finding excuses to talk to her quietly, out of the hearing of the rest of us.

They're talking about the *Gazette,* I told myself, but I didn't believe it.

Zack, never one to mind his own business, was reading

my gossip column over my shoulder. "This is mind-boggling stuff you've got here," he said, dropping potato-chip crumbs all over my hair.

I shoved him away. "Zack, you are such a pig. Get away from me or chew with your mouth closed."

He ignored me. "What's this hot item right here? 'Muffin McCarthy's daddy is giving her a trip to Aspen this winter as a reward for losing those big bad ten pounds she put on over the summer. Congratulations, Muffin!'" Zack pretended to collapse into his chair.

"Help!" he croaked. "Are we ready for hard news like this?"

"I'm doing the best I can!" I yelled. "If you don't like it, write the gossip column yourself."

Zack emptied the potato-chip bag into his hand and dumped all the crumbs into his mouth at once. "Where's your cartoon?"

I shoved it across the table and watched him raise his eyebrows. "Trumpet might not like that," he said.

Lucie overheard us and joined Zack at the table. She shook her head slowly over my cartoon. "I love it, Teddy, but it could get you into big trouble."

I had drawn the old maple tree lying on the lawn and labeled it "The Good Old Days." It wasn't by any means the best cartoon I'd ever done, so I was surprised at their reaction.

"He's going to take it personally," Lucie said.

"Yeah," Zack laughed. "You ought to draw in a termite and name it Trumpet."

I pretended to reach for my pen, and both Lucie and Zack yelled, "Stop!"

Laughing, I took back my cartoon. "He won't notice, and neither will anyone else. They'll all think I meant that the good old days were when all those initials were carved on the tree."

"Maybe," Lucie said doubtfully. "But I think it's more

75

likely that everyone will know you meant the good old days before Mr. Trumpteller came here."

"The feature page is mine," I argued, "and I'm putting this cartoon in."

"It's your funeral, too," Zack said.

Fine and Devon had joined us at my end of the table and looked at the cartoon without comment. Sure patted my shoulder. It seemed to me that we were getting to be a pretty morbid bunch.

A few minutes later the twins took off with Zack, and Lucie disappeared, too. I gathered my stuff together, anxious to get away from Devon. I felt very self-conscious around him. He hadn't said much of anything to me that day, and I hadn't had any sort of conversation with him since Saturday night, when he kissed me. The more I thought about it, the more I was sure that he had asked me to go to the dance with him only because Fine was busy. I didn't want him to know how miserable I was.

"I've got my dad's car," Devon said suddenly. "Do you want a ride home? It's still raining."

I was tempted to say no, just to show him how independent I was, but that would have been dumb. Who turns down a ride when it's raining?

"Sure," I said. "Thanks."

The student parking lot was nearly empty, and we made a dash for it, running as fast as we could through the rain. But just as we got to the car, Devon let out a yell.

"The hubcaps are gone!"

Both of us stood there, rain streaming down our faces, and stared at the tires as if they could explain the situation to us.

"My dad is going to kill me," Devon said angrily.

"Who do you suppose did it?" I asked. It was a stupid question. How could Devon know?

"Somebody who wanted new hubcaps, of course. Well,

get in and I'll take you home. We aren't going to find them by standing here and drowning in the rain."

I opened the door on the passenger side and was about to get in when I heard Trumpet yelling from the school door. You could have heard him for ten miles.

"What's going on out there?" he bellowed. "Is there some kind of trouble?"

He came loping out, carrying a big black umbrella in one hand and a briefcase in the other. Then I saw that his own car was parked in the student parking lot again. For a minute I had the crazy, happy hope that maybe his hubcaps also had been stolen.

"What's this? What's this?" he fussed as he trotted up to us.

"Someone took my dad's hubcaps," Devon said.

Trumpet circled the car, examining each tire as if he didn't believe Devon. "You're right," he said fretfully. "They're gone."

Devon slid into the driver's seat and would have closed the car door, but Trumpet wasn't done yet. "Who did this?" he demanded.

He actually expected us to know, I guess. Devon and I exchanged glances and shrugged.

"You must have *some* idea," Trumpet insisted. "We've got to stop this vandalism. Teddy! You know everyone in the school. Who would do such a thing?"

I shook my head. Having lived in Catherwood all my life didn't mean that I'd know who would go around stealing hubcaps.

"Excuse me, Mr. Trumpteller, but I've got to go," Devon said impatiently, starting the car. Trumpet nodded, grudgingly giving his assent, and we drove away in silence. When I looked back, I saw Trumpet stalking toward his car and trying to keep his umbrella from blowing away.

Devon's silence bothered me. "I'm sorry," I said. "I

really have no idea who would have done a stupid thing like that."

"I know," he said. "I didn't think you did."

He didn't say anything more than good-bye when I got out of the car, and I didn't even consider asking him to come in the house. He seemed worried about what his dad would think, and I didn't blame him.

So what could have been a cozy ride in a car during a storm fizzled out totally. I didn't know any more than I knew before about how Devon felt. I looked up at the sky as I went up the porch steps, half expecting to see the great cosmic bad-luck machine hanging up there, humming and buzzing happily to itself.

Gotcha, Teddy!

Chapter Twelve

THE NEXT DAY I was standing in the lunch line between Lucie and Jo-Sue, discussing the rumor that Miss Bilky might leave the hospital early, when Zack came skidding up, all out of breath. He looked as if the world had just come to an end.

"You oughta see the parking lot! It's the biggest mess. Cliff Park's dad is here and wants to call the police, but Trumpet doesn't want him to. Devon is interviewing the kids whose cars got it the worst."

"What?" Lucie asked. "There's more trouble? I can't take any more trouble." Right there, as I watched, her nose turned red and she sneezed three times in a row.

"What are you yelling about?" I asked Zack.

He looked at us as if he'd been telling a sensible story and we were just too stupid to understand. "Someone's trashed all the cars. You've got to see it!"

We left the line and followed him outside. I never saw such a mess in my life. There were probably twenty or thirty cars in the lot, and every one of them had been trashed. All of them had been splashed with white paint, and three of the cars closest to the lawn had had their tires slashed. One had a broken window in the passenger door. I was so stunned that I didn't know what to say.

"See?" Zack cried. "I told you so."

A big crowd of kids had gathered around Trumpet and a tall, gray-haired man, so we walked over to see what was going on. I could see Devon, notebook in hand, talking to several boys near the cars with the slashed tires. Everyone looked angry, especially the gray-haired man with Trumpet.

"I want the police here, and I'm not going to argue with you anymore," Mr. Park said. He turned and walked away suddenly, as if he'd had about all he could take of the situation.

"But we can handle everything," Trumpet called after him. "We'll find out who did this."

Mr. Park didn't even slow down. He turned the corner and headed toward the police station two blocks up the street. Catherwood had never had so much excitement. Chief McMillan was probably going to have a stroke. For him a big day was when someone made an illegal left turn in front of Dwyer's Department Store.

Lucie, Jo-Sue, and I hung around for a while, watching and waiting for developments. Zack had joined Devon, and neither of them even looked up when we walked past. Devon was writing as fast as he could and Zack was reading over his shoulder, nodding emphatically. We went back into the building just as Chief McMillan drove up in his police car with Mr. Park.

"Wow!" Jo-Sue pawed at her hair. "Who do you suppose did it?"

"Someone crazy," Lucie said. "It can't be one of the students here. I don't know anyone who'd do something like that."

I must have been in shock. Sometimes I think that Catherwood is a boring little town—we don't even have our own movie theater—but my folks are right. When a town is this small, everyone watches everyone else and not as many bad things happen. Nothing this awful had happened for as long as I could remember.

The cafeteria had emptied out by the time we got back. I guess everyone had gone outside to stare, except the monitors—they weren't allowed to leave their posts until lunch period was over, and they looked ready to come unglued.

"What's going on?" one of them asked.

"Somebody messed up the cars in the student parking lot," I told him. "Where were all the monitors when everything was happening?"

"There aren't any monitors for the parking lot," he said. "But I'll ask Mr. Trumpteller. Maybe he'll assign some of us out there." He puffed up his chest. "He could have used us."

He was right, I suppose, but I didn't much like people who volunteered to spy, so I didn't say anything to him. We got our sandwiches and went to our favorite table, wondering what would happen next.

It was a crazy day. By the time the last class was out, only three or four cars were left in the parking lot. You could see where someone had tried to wipe the white paint off one of the cars, making the mess worse by smearing it. I walked around the parking lot with Zack for a few minutes, then we went to the *Gazette* office and talked to Devon. He read his notes to us, but we didn't learn anything new from him. Everyone was upset, and no one had a clue about who could have done such a rotten thing.

I hated to admit it, but something had been bothering me. I hadn't seen Billy anywhere in school that day, and usually I caught at least a glimpse of him. His absence was beginning to get to me. I know I have an overactive imagination—I've been told that enough times—but I was beginning to wonder if Billy had trashed the cars.

I'll explain why. He had all those penalty hours, and he must have been angry, even if he didn't show it. And he was an outsider, even though he'd lived in Catherwood all his life. He didn't have any close friends except for Zack and me. He just sort of hung around the edges of things, and lately he'd seemed even more remote and odd. Not angry or anything like that. Just odd.

I decided I must be cracking up from the strain. I'd known Billy forever, and he'd never done anything really awful. Never.

Somebody, a stranger, had done it, and we'd probably never find out who it was. Last year there'd been a problem in the parking lot, and we never found out who was responsible. The same person had probably come back and done it again, only worse this time. That was the answer, of course.

But I was worried about Billy all the same. I had an awful hunch that he was going to be first on Trumpet's list of suspects.

All of us on the *Gazette* staff decided that we needed a night out together to cheer ourselves up, so we had dinner again at the pizza place. We were all on second helpings when Devon rapped his glass with a spoon.

"Attention!" he said. "I think that we deserve a special treat tonight."

"You're right." Zack reached for a menu. "Let's order another pizza and two desserts."

"No, I mean something else," Devon said. "Why don't I call my sister and see if she can get passes again? There's a good movie showing. How about it? The best part is that it's free."

We all agreed, so Devon went off to the phone and came back grinning. "It's on. We can pick up the passes at the box office. The movie starts in half an hour, so we'd better get going."

We all piled into Zack's old station wagon and headed for the theater. I sat next to Devon, and Fine was in front with Zack. Lucie and Sure began to sing, and for a while I forgot about Billy.

We had a great time, considering everything. Even though Devon didn't say anything particularly personal to me that evening, he didn't single Fine out either. Maybe he really did like me best but didn't want to hurt Fine's feelings by showing it. I hugged that thought to myself.

We loved the movie, and I was home by eleven. Stubbornly, I refused even to think that I'd only been one of the gang to Devon that night. He must have been thinking about me during the movie, because I had been thinking about him so hard that my head ached.

My folks were watching an old movie on TV, so Dominic and I went up to my room without disturbing them. I was exhausted from all the excitement, so I didn't waste much time getting ready for bed. I was just about to crawl under the blankets when I thought of Billy again, and I went to the window and looked down at the street below.

I honestly hoped I wouldn't see him there. I wanted to believe that he was home with Cal and his dad, watching TV, or maybe just sitting around talking.

But Billy stood under the streetlight again, looking at our front porch. His hands were in his pockets, and his shoulders were hunched against the cold.

Oh, Billy, I thought. Can't you take better care of yourself? You're getting into terrible trouble, and you don't seem to care. What's going to happen to you? I crawled into bed, shivering.

And what's going to happen to me? I thought. Does Devon care about me or not?

Sometimes I wished that life could be like a book and I could be like Jo-Sue. She always looked at the last page to see how a story ended before she began reading. Curled up in a ball in my cold bed, I wanted to see how the story of Devon and Teddy ended.

Chapter Thirteen

"ONE MORE DAY to go," I said to Zack that Tuesday morning in the *Gazette* office. "Let's all hold our breath and keep our fingers crossed that the paper will be better this time."

Zack wasn't that worried. He'd done his best to jazz up the sports page, and now all he had to do was gather up everything and be ready to go with Miss Lamb, the librarian, to the printer on Wednesday.

"Are you still turning in that cartoon showing the old tree blown down?" he asked me.

"Sure." The more I thought about it, the better I liked it.

"Have you finished the gossip column?" Lucie called over to me. She was sitting at her desk, drinking a cup of lukewarm tea and working her way through a box of tissues. Her allergies were worse than ever.

"All done, and boring enough to satisfy Trumpet and his grandmother."

Lucie sighed and went back to the pile of junk on her desk. The twins and Devon had scattered pages all over the table, and the three of them were hissing at each other about something. Mean as I am, I was glad to see that Fine and Devon didn't always get along.

Their major problem seemed to be that Devon wanted to do things the way he'd done them at his last school, which wasn't the way we did them at the *Gazette*. None of this bothered Zack or me, because we didn't write for the general news page, but the twins were going crazy. If there was one thing Devon was stubborn about, it was the front page.

"Let's let Lucie decide," Sure said, giving Devon an exasperated look.

Lucie sighed again and blew her nose violently. "I'm not going to waste time settling every little squabble you three have."

"Devon is general news editor for now, so what he says goes," Zack announced, and both twins made faces at him. The same face, actually. How could they not be related? It was amazing.

"And if Zack says something, it must be true," Devon laughed. Things lightened up a little after that. Devon had the knack for smoothing things over that Zack and I lacked. Sometimes we made things worse. But even though Devon was a real diplomat, I noticed that he got his own way often enough.

No doubt about it, Devon fit in just fine with us. I was certain that when Miss Bilky got back, she'd see to it that Devon stayed on as general news editor. And Trumpet wasn't going to complain—I could already see that our principal was crazy about jocks. Devon wasn't going to do Catherwood's reputation any harm during track season.

I watched him as he worked with his hair falling over his forehead and a serious look on his face. He was gorgeous. And interested in me. A little bit, anyway. At least we spent lots of time together. I should have been satisfied while I was ahead.

"Girls!" Zack said disgustedly. He'd seen me watching Devon.

"Don't come around begging at lunch today," I warned him. "I didn't bring any dog biscuits."

When the first bell rang, we all headed toward our classes. The hall monitors were busier than ever, it seemed. They had eyes in the backs of their heads and noticed anyone trying to sneak cinnamon rolls out of the cafeteria or slamming locker doors shut without locking them. It was depressing.

In spite of all this, we had to admit that the halls were cleaner and quieter. A lot cleaner and a lot quieter.

After first period I saw Billy in the main hall and ran to catch up with him. He looked as if he didn't have a care in the world, and he had another science fiction book tucked under his arm.

"How come you weren't in school yesterday?" I asked.

He grinned at me. "I had other plans."

"Did you hear about what happened in the student parking lot?"

"Sure. What a mess."

He was acting as if the vandalism were something that had happened on Mars. Couldn't Billy see he was in a lot of trouble? It would be so easy for someone like Trumpet to blame Billy for everything.

He turned off the main hall then and took the stairs up to the second floor. He waved once and grinned as if nothing in the world were wrong.

Lucie had a lunchtime appointment with her advisor, and Jo-Sue had to go to the dentist, so I ended up alone at our table, chewing one of Mom's date-nut-fig-orange-pit specials and wondering why I was so cranky if this was supposed to be the best part of my life.

My feet felt especially big that day, no doubt due to the orange pits in Mom's diet bar. I'd lost all my enthusiasm for working on the *Gazette,* my beige wool skirt was decorated with Dominic's hair, and my personality was all wrong. And right across the room from me, Fine and Devon were whispering together again.

I couldn't stand to watch, so I opened a book and pretended to read. Zack flopped down next to me after a while, eating his way through a meat-loaf sandwich and shedding crumbs everywhere. "Did you hear?" he asked.

"Hear what?"

"Someone let the air out of Trumpet's tires again. And this time his car was in the faculty parking lot." Zack seemed awfully pleased.

I shut my book. "Were the other cars okay?"

"Yes. Who do you suppose is doing this stuff?"

Without thinking I said, "Whoever has the most penalty hours."

"Billy." Zack chewed thoughtfully for a moment. "But Billy isn't nuts, and a nut has to be doing this."

I glanced up and saw Fine and Devon leaving the cafeteria. "No, Billy wouldn't trash cars. Who do you think is doing it?"

Zack brushed crumbs off his shirt and onto me. "How about one of the freshmen?"

"Not likely."

"Maybe one of the monitors has gone berserk. You know, absolute power corrupts and all that stuff."

I stared at Zack. "Where do you get these crazy ideas?"

He took off his glasses and crossed his eyes. "I watch a lot of TV."

I punched his arm. "Quit doing that. You're making me seasick."

He slipped his glasses back on and suddenly looked very serious. "Why don't we get together and talk about this? We could go out for pizza all by ourselves. Or maybe have a real dinner somewhere. What do you think?"

I gawked at him. Was he asking me for a real date? Zack? Or was this another one of his miserable jokes?

"Well, I mean, you don't have a steady," he went on. "And you never go out with Billy, even though he's crazy about you. And Devon seems to be more interested in Fine than he is in you." Zack peered at me through his glasses, and he looked desperate. He also had no tact.

"Thanks a heap," I said sourly. "Do you think I'll go out with you if you insult me enough? Why don't you just say that no one else will ask me out because my feet are too big?"

Zack bent down and looked under the table. "Good night, Matilda! They really are big, aren't they? Maybe I'd better reconsider my offer. I'm not sure you could get those boxcars in the front seat. You might have to let them drag alongside."

I couldn't help starting to laugh, and before long Zack was laughing, too. Everyone stared at us, and one of the monitors came bustling over.

"Trouble?" he asked, leering at me.

"Clear out of here, Brookwalter, before I flatten your face!" Zack yelled.

The monitor wandered off, not quite sure what he should do. I didn't think any of Trumpet's guidelines included the exact number of demerits for laughing. Not yet, anyway.

I ended up telling Zack that I didn't think my folks would be crazy about my going out on a weeknight, especially since I was behind in my homework. I invited him to my place for dinner—not that he hadn't been there before. And he must have forgotten about my mother's cooking, because he accepted immediately and even walked me to my next class.

During sixth period we got another shock. Trumpet made an announcement over the PA system: The student parking lot was closed until further notice, and the faculty parking lot was restricted.

There were a lot of groans from the kids who drove to school. The idea seemed sensible to me, but I didn't say anything out loud. It was hard for me to admit to myself that sometimes Trumpet was right. He did so many dumb things, though, that the good ones were canceled out. In a lot of ways he was as awkward as the freshmen—he tried too hard.

88

That evening Zack came over for dinner, all dressed up in a tweed jacket. He looked so neat and tidy that Dominic didn't recognize him and barked up a storm.

"Would you like to watch the news with me?" Dad asked Zack.

I'm sure Zack remembered that Dad yells at the TV set during the news—and other times, too—but he marched off bravely. Mom and I went into the kitchen.

Maybe it was out of pity, but Mom fixed plain old fried chicken that night instead of smothering the chicken with cracked soybeans and boiled spinach. Dinner was a great success, and Dad restrained himself from explaining why I'm named Teddy. He loves to tell that story, unfortunately. Or maybe Zack had heard it before. I couldn't remember, but in any event, I was proud of all of us.

I was more than proud of Zack. I guess I'd been taking him for granted since we were little kids, and I never expected much from him except lots of laughs. But that night he seemed different somehow. Good-looking and cool. And, well, older, I guess. I tried not to stare at him, but I honestly felt as if I hardly knew him. I could tell that my folks were really impressed with him, and that relieved my mind. Before dinner I'd been worrying that Zack would pull one of his really far-out stunts. But he didn't.

Once, when he looked over at me and smiled, I felt myself blush. Over Zack? I asked myself. Come on, Teddy, you're having some sort of hallucination.

He went home about nine o'clock, and Mom and I went back to the kitchen to clean up.

"He's a nice boy," Mom said, scraping baked-potato skins into Dominic's pan. "There've been times, though, when I thought he was a little bit strange."

"He's not strange," I said defensively. "Well, maybe sometimes. But I know people who are lot worse. Billy, for instance."

I shouldn't have mentioned his name. Mom immediately got all dewy-eyed. "Billy is not strange. He's sensitive. Wounded by life." She must have liked that expression, because she repeated it several times while she got Dominic's bowl ready.

"Billy might be in trouble at school," I said.

"Never. Billy's just independent. He'd never get into real trouble."

I gave up. If I'd hoped for any serious help with the problem from Mom, I was mistaken. She wouldn't be able to see Billy as anything but lost, lonely, and one step away from sainthood.

Long after Zack left, I sat in my room thinking. Billy was on my mind too much. It was as if I was haunted by him. The more I thought about things, the more possible it seemed that Billy could be the one vandalizing the parking lot. I could even see him doing it, moving between the cars in that quiet, smiling way of his. Splashing paint. Letting air out of tires.

But what I couldn't see him doing was actually destroying things—car windows, for instance. Or slashing tires.

I looked for Billy, but he wasn't standing across the street that night, and I was glad. I lay awake thinking about Devon instead, wondering if he had spent the evening with Fine.

And why shouldn't he have? I'd spent the evening with Zack, after all.

But that was different. Zack and I were friends, and we had everything in common. Zack didn't spoil things the way Billy did by caring too much about me, even though he *had* more or less asked me for a date. Maybe that had been a momentary mental slip.

Whatever was going on between Devon and Fine, however, could not be called simple friendship.

Chapter Fourteen

THE *GAZETTE* CAME out on Friday, and it was a total dud. Again.

One thing I can say about the kids at Catherwood High —they never leave you in the dark about how they feel. On my way to the cafeteria at noon I saw one of the kids crumple up his copy of the paper and throw it on the floor. A hall monitor caught him in the act and gave him a demerit.

"It was worth it," the kid said, glaring at me. The big old cosmic bad-luck machine was right on target.

I stopped by the *Gazette* office to see if Lucie was going to eat there or in the cafeteria. "What'll it be?" I asked. "Public humiliation or private pain?"

"I'm never going to eat again," Lucie said, blowing her nose on a paper towel. I was shocked at her condition. She looked as if she had two black eyes.

"All this is because of your allergies?" I asked. I'd never realized that anyone could get that sick from things that don't bother the rest of us.

She scowled at me. "Mr. Trumpteller called me out of my third-period class, and I sneezed in his office twenty-three times. He told me to go home because I was spreading germs and was going to cause an epidemic at school. He actually sprayed his office with disinfectant while I was standing there."

"Allergies aren't catching!"

"Try to tell *him* that. I could have died, I was so embarrassed." She honked her nose again.

"What did he think about the paper?"

"Oh," Lucie said happily, "he's going to kill you as soon as he sees you, that's all."

I leaned against the table. "He said that?"

"He used words to that effect. If I were you, I'd leave town. He didn't like the cartoon, and I think he was the only one in school to get the point of it. Honestly, Teddy, you are the most tactless girl I ever knew."

Oh, well. Trumpet could murder me only once, I told myself. "I'm going to the cafeteria to eat something gross and fattening. Are you sure you won't come along?" I asked.

"Get out of here before I kill you myself," Lucie said quietly, and I believed her. She was desperate.

When I got to the cafeteria, Devon and Zack were sitting together and sharing a hamburger. They didn't look too happy either. "Everybody hates the *Gazette*," Devon said. Even scowling he was cute, but I didn't want him scowling at me.

"Look, we did the best we could."

"The paper is a bore, Teddy," Zack said. "And I did my best to hide the list of penalty-hall kids in the back, but everybody saw it, and now we look like real jerks. I'm tired of explaining that it wasn't my idea to put their names in the paper."

"Gee," I said, appalled, "I just assumed you'd 'forget' it."

"Are you kidding? Trumpet wouldn't let me forget it!"

I sat down across from them and dropped my books on the floor. "Did anyone say anything nice?"

"Sure," Zack replied, laughing. "Some of the kids liked the ad page." He shoved a copy of the *Gazette* toward me. "Take a look."

I hadn't even seen the back page that morning, so I

flipped the paper over and studied it. Right away I saw what was wrong.

Selling ads is the responsibility of the freshman journalism class. They sold an ad to a funeral home, and it appeared right under the ad for the Catherwood Health Spa. It didn't take much imagination to draw some pretty funny conclusions.

"This is what Miss Bilky would call 'regrettable planning,'" I said, laughing.

"You may think it's funny, but I feel sorry for Miss Lamb," Devon said. "She planned the ad page, and everybody knows it."

The twins came by then. They looked devastated. "Trumpet bawled out Miss Lamb, right in the encyclopedia section."

I thought we were going to have to call an ambulance for Zack because he laughed so hard he started choking. Sure and Fine didn't think it was funny though, and Devon ended up taking Fine by the arm and leading her to the other side of the room.

Wonderful, I thought. Now he has to rescue her from us. I was having a hard time remembering that Devon had ever kissed me.

I moved to the other side of the table, and Zack and I consoled ourselves, with only Sure for company. I kept my eyes turned away from Devon and Fine. I'd had enough of them for one day.

Before lunch period was over, I got several specific complaints from people who'd given me gossip items about themselves. They were disappointed that I hadn't included their gems. I explained that I had limited space, but that didn't help. They were mad.

It was too much to hope that I'd get through the day without running into Trumpet, although I did my best. He cornered me just before sixth period, and right there in the hall, for everyone to hear and appreciate, he said, "I hoped you would see how important it is for the *Gazette* to support my efforts in correcting the problems here."

You could have heard a fly tap-dance in that hall. The kids around us were creeping past, not looking at us.

"I'm sorry," I offered, although I really wasn't the least bit sorry. I was furious that he would talk to me in front of all the kids hurrying to their last classes. The monitors were absolutely gloating.

"Where's your friend?" he asked suddenly.

I thought he meant Devon. I guess I'd been thinking about him just before Trumpet caught me. "I suppose he's in gym."

"What?"

"Devon's in gym now."

"Not Devon. I meant Billy. I know he's a good friend of yours."

I knew that Billy should have been in his German class and that he probably wasn't. But why was I being held responsible for his whereabouts?

"I don't know where Billy is, and I'm going to be late for class." With an impatient wave of his hand, Trumpet indicated our conversation was over. I started walking away just as the last bell rang, and I was too angry and proud to ask Trumpet for a hall pass that would let me into my class and spare me a demerit. Lucie would have called me stubborn.

I couldn't concentrate for the rest of the day. I was losing my enthusiasm for working on the *Gazette,* even though it had been the best part of school for me—and had given me an excuse to see Devon regularly.

But what was the point? Devon was obviously interested in Fine, not me. If I'd learned anything at all, it was that you couldn't do anything about a problem like that except watch it happen.

I didn't stop by the *Gazette* office after school. Instead,

I grabbed my coat from my locker and ran out, not speaking to anyone. I needed to think.

I hurried across the empty student parking lot, heading for home just as fast as I could. I didn't see Billy until he caught up with me.

"What's the rush?"

I turned on him furiously. "I hope you know that you got me in trouble this afternoon. Trumpet was looking for you. He seems to think that I'm responsible for you."

Billy took my books, jerking them out of my hands because I wouldn't let go of them at first. I was even sick and tired of his old-fashioned good manners.

"He called me out of German class," Billy told me. "But I had an alibi for the time someone was letting the air out of his tires." His grin was resigned and sweet.

"I knew you didn't do it," I said. Suddenly, all my anger was gone. Billy has a calming effect on me sometimes.

He matched his steps with mine. "Well, Trumpet still thinks I did it, along with everything else that's happened around here. He just can't prove it."

"He's been mad at you from the first day he saw you. He didn't like the way you stood up for Dominic and me."

"I gave Dominic to you, so in a way he's partly my dog. And I wish you were my girl." His words just slipped out, quietly and smoothly, and when I looked at Billy, he didn't seem at all sorry.

Here it was. The moment I dreaded, but the one I knew would come. "I can't be your girl," I whispered. "We've always been friends, and I can't think of you as anything else. Not the way you mean, anyway."

There. It was out. I'd turned my head away while I was speaking, and now I looked back at Billy. He was staring straight ahead, with no expression on his face, but I knew he heard me.

"I know," he said softly.

Neither of us said anything more. After a block or so, I

noticed that Cal was skulking along behind us again. I decided to be kind. I'd given Billy enough to be sad about for one day.

"How's Cal been?"

"He's had the flu or something. This is the first day he's been back at school," Billy replied. "I don't think he feels very well yet, but Dad said it would be okay for him to get out of bed. I guess he got pretty bored staying at home."

"Then he likes school better than he did?"

Billy shrugged. "I guess he likes it as well as anybody can like school."

"Listen—" I began.

"Don't lecture me today," Billy interrupted. "I don't like school the way you do. I wish I had a job or was old enough to join the Navy."

"You have to graduate from high school first," I told him. "Remember the Navy recruiter who was here last year? I'm sure that's what he said."

"I could pass an equivalency test."

Fat chance, I thought. Even though Billy was smart, he barely got through his classes. "School isn't as bad as you think it is. We have fun too, you know."

"*You* have fun. I don't," Billy said quietly.

What he said was true enough. I never understood why Billy seemed so out of place at school. But that was how things were with him. I was beginning to suspect that it hurt me more than it hurt him.

We were home by then, and Billy came in for a while to visit with Mom and the dog. Both of them were happy to see him. When I passed the living-room window, I saw Cal leaning against the fence outside. I went back to the door and called to him to come in. He stared at me without blinking and then shook his head. I was going to say something more, to coax him a little, but suddenly he turned and ran off.

Billy left just before Dad got home. Dominic rushed out

the back door the minute the front door closed behind Billy, and Mom and I started dinner preparations. As we were putting things on the table, the front doorbell rang, and I heard Dad answer it.

A moment later, he came into the kitchen. "That was you-know-who from next door," he said, scowling. "It seems that Dominic is outside the fence, and she is going to call the police if we don't do something. I have half a mind to leave him out there for the rest of the evening."

"I'll get him," I volunteered. I knew that Dad hated to wrestle with Dominic in public. It was pretty undignified trying to get a monster dog up off his back and moving in the general direction of the porch. I hurried out and poked my sleeping dog. "Up, you moron."

He groaned and squinted his eyes shut, trying to pretend he was still asleep.

"Don't you know you shouldn't be out here? Dogs should be inside fences, where they're safe."

Dominic mumbled to himself as he climbed the steps, trying to tell me, I guess, that a dog his size was perfectly safe anywhere. I supposed he was sulking again because Billy left. Everyone loved Billy.

Except me.

But I did love him, in my own way. I loved him the way sisters love brothers. Or the way I loved Jo-Sue and Lucie.

I didn't feel about Billy the way I did about Devon. In spite of all the disappointments in my relationship with Devon, I still thought about him constantly. I watched for him wherever I went. When the phone rang I hoped it would be him. I even chose clothes I thought he'd like me to wear.

And for the first time in my life I was beginning to hate myself, because I didn't seem to be the kind of girl Devon wanted.

Chapter Fifteen

LUCIE AND I visited Miss Bilky on Saturday and heard her good news. She would be leaving the hospital in just a few more days. "But I'll be stuck at home for a long time," she said. "I don't know how I'll stand it."

"We'll come by your apartment and fill you in on everything," Lucie offered.

"I'm not certain that I'll want to hear it. How are things going?"

Lucie and I exchanged a quick glance. "Not too bad, all things considered," I told her.

Miss Bilky sank back on her pillows with a big sigh. "That's what I was afraid of."

We would have been stuck for something cheerful to say if Zack and Devon hadn't come in then.

"Here, light of my life," Zack said as he handed Miss Bilky a big, greasy paper sack.

She opened it and grinned. "Oh, you remembered!" She passed the sack to us. Zack had brought her a whole dozen of those big drippy doughnuts from the bakery across the street from school. Who would have thought that someone as elegant as Miss Bilky would even have touched one of those things, much less eat it?

Lucie and I told her that we'd just had huge breakfasts and couldn't manage to swallow another bite. That wasn't exactly true, but there weren't many times that I'd been hungry enough to eat one of those doughnuts.

Zack and Devon each took one and Miss Bilky was left with the rest. She dug right in.

We stayed with her for an hour, mostly gossiping about school, and everyone worked hard to avoid mentioning the *Gazette*. Not one of us had brought her a copy. There's no point in going out of your way to make someone miserable.

Afterward, Lucie left to see her allergy specialist again, although I couldn't see what good all those shots were doing her.

"If I didn't take them, I might be even worse," she explained. "They aren't working because of all the stress. At least that's what the doctor said."

We were standing together outside the front door of the hospital, with Zack and Devon hanging around, probably waiting to see what we were planning to do.

"Doesn't last year seem like paradise when you think about it?" I asked. "How could things have been so nice and we didn't appreciate it?"

"Are you two going to stand here complaining all day, or are we going to make plans to do something exciting?" Zack protested.

"I'm too sick even to think about doing exciting things," Lucie said. "But just in case, what did you have in mind?"

"How about pizza before the game?"

"What game?" I asked.

Zack looked horrified. *"Our* game. This is Saturday, you dimwit. Good old Catherwood High is taking on Beaver Falls." He poked up his glasses and stared at me. "Don't tell me you weren't going to go?"

"That seems to be what I'm telling you. You know I don't like football."

Zack reeled away from me as if he were about to faint.

Lucie flatly refused to eat pizza again for lunch and said good-bye. That left Devon, Zack, and me together at the curb.

"I don't want pizza either. I want to go for a walk," I said.

"Walk! I'm too hungry to walk," Zack complained.

"Tell you what," Devon proposed. "You go eat your pizza, Zack, and I'll meet you outside the stadium before the game. Meanwhile, I'll walk Teddy home."

Zack thought we were crazy, but he agreed. Devon and I started for my house, at least two miles away.

The weather was perfect for a long walk. The late September sun was warm enough to make us uncomfortable wearing our jackets, so we carried them, and when we reached the park, we decided to cut through it.

There's an old bandstand in the middle of the park, and we sat down for a while on one of the benches. I wished time would stop right then so I could be happy forever.

"Do they really have concerts here?" Devon asked.

"Sure," I told him. "But not as often as they did when I was a little girl. We used to have picnics here on Sundays and listen to the music."

"I bet you were cute when you were little," Devon said, taking my hand. "You're still cute. But you aren't so little."

"Don't bring that up," I told him. "I hate being reminded of how tall I am."

"You aren't as tall as I am."

I thought we looked great together, but I decided not to say anything out loud. I wasn't sure how he felt about Fine and I didn't want to set myself up to hear the same speech I had given Billy. I knew I must have hurt him. Just thinking about it made me miserable.

"What was the big sigh for?" Devon asked.

"Oh, nothing. I'm in a good mood, really."

"You usually are, even when you're working on the paper. But then, the whole *Gazette* staff is great. The last paper I worked on wasn't much fun. I think we spent more time rewriting our stuff than you guys do. Nothing we did was ever right the first time. Or even the fifth time." He laughed a little and stretched his long legs. "Our journalism teacher ended up writing practically everything herself."

"Miss Bilky's not like that. She pretty much lets us do things our own way."

"That's what I thought. You all seem to have fun working on the *Gazette*. Patty likes it, too."

"Patty?" Who was he talking about?

"You know—Fine. You've all been calling her Fine for so long that you've forgotten what her real name is." His grin dazzled me.

Devon was right. Her name *was* Patty, but I don't think anyone had called her that since she and Sure had shown up their first day. From the expression on his face, I could tell that he liked her more than I wanted him to.

"You and Fine—I mean Patty—see a lot of each other, don't you?" I blurted.

Devon slid down on the bench, so relaxed that he looked as if he were made out of rubber. "She's nice. Sorta calm and quiet, but I like that. She has a good sense of humor, too."

"That's true." What else could I say? A small cold knot settled in my chest. If there was anything I wasn't, it was calm and quiet. No one had to tell me that. I was too noisy, too emotional, too tall, and everything else I suddenly didn't want to be. While I had sometimes wished I could be different, I had never wished it as hard as I did right then.

"Come on," Devon said unexpectedly. "If I'm going to meet Zack on time, I'd better get you home."

He pulled me to my feet and kept my hand in his as we crossed the park. I pushed all thoughts of Fine from my mind. Right now, Devon was with me, and that was what counted.

When we got to my house, we stood on the porch to-gether and he took my hand again.

"This was nice. Let's do it again sometime."

I tried not to smile like an ape. "Sure," I said in my coolest manner. "I enjoyed it, too."

I watched him walk away and then went into the house. Dad was in his den where he would spend the afternoon arguing with television football commentators and devour-ing stacks of sandwiches. Mom wasn't home, and Dominic was having his afternoon nap.

I cleaned up my bedroom and gave a lot of thought to the conversation Devon and I had had about Fine. He liked placid girls, that was obvious. So what was stopping me from being that way? I didn't have to be so enthusiastic about everything. I could pretend to have a more reserved attitude until it became second nature. I'd stop arguing with Zack over every little thing. And the next time I got mad at the Student Justice Committee, I'd do what Fine did. I'd let my eyes fill with tears and wipe them away with a neat handkerchief. I would definitely not yell and slam my books down on the *Gazette* office table. I'd make myself over to please Devon.

It sounded simple.

Jo-Sue called when she got home after the game and asked me to spend the night at her house.

"I'm in no mood to talk to anyone but you," she said.

"What's wrong?" I could tell how upset she was, and I knew without seeing her that her hair was pulled into those spiky little peaks.

"I'll tell you when you get here. I'm trying to make up my mind about something, so I really want you to come over."

I left right after dinner and found Jo-Sue in her bedroom, eating chocolate drops out of a bag and listening to her stereo. She had been crying.

"You look like the end of the world," I told her.

"That's just how I feel."

I dropped my tote and sat down in the rocking chair next to her bed. She offered me a chocolate, and I chewed while I waited. Jo-Sue likes to take her time planning what she's going to say.

"I think," she said finally, "that I'm going to have to resign from my office."

I swallowed. "You're kidding. Why would you give up being junior-class president? You're sure to be elected president of the senior class next year."

She sat up cross-legged. "I can't be on that stupid Student Justice Committee again. Do you realize how many people hate me now?"

I'd heard a few people make nasty remarks about her— behind her back—but her friends always stuck up for her. The Student Justice Committee wasn't her idea, and we knew that.

"Everyone will cool down pretty soon. You'll see. As soon as we learn all the rules, no one will be getting any more demerits. Or at least most of us won't."

"It isn't just that. It's sitting there, counting demerits, while some poor freshman, or Billy, or maybe even Zack next time stands up in front of us and waits for us to dole out penalty hours. You should see the looks on their faces, Teddy!"

She was starting to cry again, so I passed the sack of chocolate drops back to her. "Eat," I said. "You'll feel better."

She threw the sack on the floor and yanked at her hair. "I'm never going to feel better about it. Not unless I quit. I told my folks, and they said to do whatever I think is best.

But I could tell that they weren't too crazy about my serving on that committee."

I'd told my folks about the committee, too. Mom called it a Star Chamber and told me a gruesome story about trials in the Middle Ages, when people couldn't even find out who had accused them and weren't allowed to have a lawyer help them.

"Maybe you could try talking to Trumpet again."

"You joke, of course. I did try. He gave me a long lecture about elected officials and how they couldn't always do what they wanted to do but sometimes had to do what was right for everyone."

"Right!" I scoffed.

"You know how he is."

We all knew. I was glad I wasn't in her position, because I would have felt just as she did. Maybe I wouldn't have resigned my office, though. I might have given Trumpet the fight of his life. At least, the old Teddy would have.

"So what do you think you're going to do?" I asked.

Tears dripped off Jo-Sue's chin. "I'm pretty sure that I'm going to resign. I was hoping you could talk me out of it."

Oh, boy. "Look," I said, "if you feel like that, don't resign. If you don't feel tough enough to argue with Trumpet, just stick it out. The kids who are criticizing you now will forget about the whole thing soon. You'll see."

"Do you believe that?"

I rocked back and forth for a minute. "No," I said finally, "but I wish I did."

We sat together in silence for a long time, and then I jumped up.

"This makes me so darned mad that I could just . . . I don't know what! I feel like letting the air out of Trumpet's tires myself. I'd like to do something really awful, just to let him know how dumb he is."

"Calm down!" Jo-Sue shouted. "You're going to make yourself sick! This is my problem, not yours."

I sat down, suddenly remembering that I was going to try to be a new Teddy, a nice, quiet Teddy. "Sorry," I mumbled.

Jo-Sue grabbed me and gave me a big hug. "That's what I love about you. You're always on my side, and you let me know it, even if you do nearly break my eardrums sometimes."

I appreciated what she said, but she wasn't the only one with problems. One of my problems was that I got too involved with other people—and always at the top of my lungs.

And Devon liked quiet girls.

Long after Jo-Sue had talked herself out and fallen asleep, I lay awake thinking. I kept going over the times in my life when people had said things to me like "Gee, Teddy, you really keep the party going" and "We can always count on you to make us laugh." Or "Teddy is the best feature editor the *Gazette* ever had. She really stirs up a storm."

No one would ever say things like that about Fine. Except for the fact that she was so pretty, she almost disappeared into the wallpaper at parties. She never said much of anything except "Fine." She was nice, and I had always liked her. But I had never envied her until now.

The more I thought about it, the more I realized that her long silences and her way of never having a strong opinion about anything probably made boys feel at ease. Most boys, anyway.

Zack said once that he thought Fine ate vanilla pudding three times a day, and it leaked into her brain. I laughed to myself, and in the next bed, Jo-Sue groaned in her sleep.

105

Enough, I told myself. I'll think things through some other time. Even character reform works better after a good night's sleep.

I wanted to dream about Devon, but I didn't. Instead, I dreamed about the day when Billy, Zack, and I were little kids and we took an oath to be friends forever. We spit on our palms and shook hands solemnly the way eight-year-olds do.

Nobody ever told us that growing up ruins everything.

Chapter Sixteen

I DIDN'T GET home from Jo-Sue's until noon on Sunday, but I'd only had a few hours with her to practice the new cool me. Actually, it hadn't worked out too well. Jo-Sue told me I was acting as if I was coming down with the flu, and when I confided my plan to her, she laughed.

"You're straining friendship to its limits, pal," I told her.

"We all like you just the way you are, Teddy!"

"But Devon would like me better if I was more like Fine."

The two of us were eating breakfast together in Jo-Sue's kitchen, surrounded by all sorts of junk food that would gag my mom. Jo-Sue put down her sweet bun covered with strawberry goo to stare at me.

"I hope you're kidding. I like Patty well enough, but she's boring. Really boring, like plain toast. You're like taco sauce."

"Gee, dear old best friend, I don't know when I've had a more thrilling compliment," I said crossly. "Taco sauce. That sounds like something Zack would say."

"I remember," she said dreamily, "when I had a crush on Zack in ninth grade."

"So do I, but you felt a lot better when you had your tonsils out." I bit into another sweet roll.

"See? That's what I mean. Patty would never say anything like that."

"Don't remind me. That's the problem exactly. I'd say it

and she wouldn't, so Devon hangs around her all the time."

Jo-Sue poured us some of her special hot chocolate, which is really half whipped cream. "He doesn't hang around her as much as you think."

"Yes he does."

She scowled. "Listen. He's awfully cute, and he's nice, too. But don't you think that he's sort of, well, *vague?*"

She was poking around an area I wouldn't let myself think about. "I don't know what you mean."

Jo-Sue was warming up to her subject now. "He acts as if he can't make up his mind. Or as if he's waiting to see what else comes up before he decides. When I asked him if he wanted to help with the junior dance, he said he'd get back to me—three times. He never did. That's what I mean. He's not like Zack, who'd say yes or no right away. Or like Billy—"

"Who'd say no right away," I finished. We both laughed.

Her parents came in then, and we changed the subject. When I left half an hour later, Jo-Sue wished me luck with the new me, and I practiced walking serenely all the way home.

Sundays aren't very exciting during the school year, so I had plenty of time to think cool thoughts and practice quiet smiles in the mirror. Dad asked me twice if I was coming down with something, but then he gave up and went off to watch television.

"Is there anything you'd like to talk about?" Mom asked while we were making dinner together.

"What did you have in mind?" I asked suspiciously.

"Well, you seem to have some sort of problem."

I sighed as loudly as I could. "Why does everyone think something is wrong with me? I'm merely trying to approach life from a different direction."

"Ah," Mom said. She looked around the kitchen distractedly. "Did you see my book? I had it here a minute ago. I thought I'd read while the pasta cooks."

I found her book, *What's in the Closet with Poor Mary?*, tucked behind the flour canister. Mom grabbed it and sat on the kitchen stool while the pasta boiled over on the stove. I could hear my father yelling at the TV in the other room. Is it any wonder that I have a warped personality?

They left me alone for the rest of the day. By bedtime I had perfected a serene expression, complete with a small half-smile. Devon, I thought, look out!

I didn't know it, but the great cosmic bad-luck machine was positioning itself right overhead.

The first thing I found out at school on Monday was that someone had spray-painted half the windows on the first floor of the school. Second period was canceled to allow for a special assembly so that Trumpet could talk and talk about the paint on the windows and how awful it was and how something was going to have to be done before the world came to an end.

In the auditorium Zack leaned across Lucie to talk to me. "It was a stupid thing to do, but does he think we're all in on it?"

My first impulse was to snap back, "Trumpet doesn't think." But instead I smiled serenely and said, "I suppose he's doing the best he can."

"Huh?" Zack mumbled to Lucie. "What did she say?"

"Shut up, Zack," Lucie whispered.

Zack slouched in his seat and gave me odd looks out of the corner of his eye until the assembly was over.

"What's wrong with you?" he asked as he followed me up the aisle. "Are you sick?"

I longed to punch his arm until he howled, but I simply shook my head. "Everything will work out just fine."

"Is she sick?" I heard him ask Lucie before the crowd in

the hall swallowed me up. I went quietly to my second class.

By lunchtime I had a headache. I don't know whether I got it because I was trying to be an ice princess or whether it developed because my third-period class was on the ground floor and the building custodians were scraping paint from the windows with razor blades, which sounded like a thousand fingernails being pulled down a thousand chalkboards. In any event, I didn't have an appetite.

Jo-Sue was already at our table when I got to the cafeteria, whispering with Zack. When I sat down they stopped, and Zack scuttled across the room to the table where he sometimes sat with Devon.

"What was all that about?" I asked Jo-Sue.

"Aren't you eating?" She looked at my tray, which held only a glass of orange juice.

Remembering the new Teddy, I said, "I'm not very hungry." I didn't entertain her with vivid descriptions of the extent of my headache or my expectation of dying before the day was out. I was sure they'd been talking about me.

She poked at her sandwich and shoved the plate away. "I'm not hungry either. I lost my appetite on my way down here when I saw Billy going into Trumpet's office."

"What?" The old Teddy was back. I was angry before I even knew what was going on.

"Billy had to see Trumpet. Do you know Monica Bell?" I nodded.

"She works in the office during third period. She said that Trumpet called in Billy and two other boys to question them about the paint."

"Billy wouldn't do something like that," I said hotly. Then I remembered that I was supposed to be serene no matter what, and I lowered my voice. "He really wouldn't."

110

"I know that," Jo-Sue protested. "You don't have to defend him to me. But Trumpet's on his case now."

"Is that what you and Zack were talking about?"

She rescued her sandwich and examined it cautiously, not looking at me. "No. We were just wishing everything could have stayed the way it used to be."

I didn't believe her. However, the new Teddy was adaptable, so I said, "Who knows, we might even like this year once things have settled down."

"Ha," she said.

Lucie joined us. Her eyes were nearly swollen shut and her nose was so red it looked as it were on fire. "Did you know that Mr. Trumpteller's after Billy again?"

We nodded and sighed together.

Lucie ate her soup quickly without a word until her bowl was empty. Then, surprisingly, she said, "I'll be glad when this year is over. I thought my senior year would be fun, but I'm beginning to hate it. Every day something new and awful happens."

"The halls are cleaner," I offered. "And remember how disgusted we used to get when kids started throwing food around here in the cafeteria?" I was trying hard.

"And remember when we had a full staff on the *Gazette* and someone else did the gossip column?" Lucie said.

"And remember—" Jo-Sue began.

"Oh, stop with the remembering!" I cried. "I'm just trying to look at this mess as positively as I can. What good is it going to do if I work myself up into a convulsion over everything?"

"But you *always* work yourself up into a convulsion over everything," Lucie said. "That's why we love you."

There I was, trying hard to look at things in a new way, and they didn't appreciate my efforts at all. But Devon might.

However, I was beginning to feel a little foolish.

I caught up with Billy in the hall before fifth period. He didn't seem too anxious to talk to me.

"I heard you got called into Trumpet's office. What was that all about?"

Billy shrugged and smiled his lazy little-boy smile, but he seemed to want some distance between us. "He's all worked up over the paint job on the windows," he said. "No big deal."

"Does he think you did it?" I pursued.

"He wishes it had been me." Billy laughed softly. "It would make his job easier." He definitely backed away from me then. "I've gotta go. See you later, Teddy."

He turned and was gone, just like that. I guess I had hurt him so much that he didn't even want to talk to me in the hall.

I had handled the whole thing wrong. I should have found some other way of telling him that we could only be friends. Or maybe I shouldn't have told him at all. I was afraid now that he would never walk home with me again.

When I got to the *Gazette* office after school, Devon was the only one there. Lucie had left a note taped to the door telling us that there would be no after-school meeting that day, but she didn't give a reason. I was sorry about that, but the cancellation gave me a chance to talk to Devon alone for a while.

He was sitting at the table, sorting through a stack of papers, and I pulled out the chair across from him.

"Have you got any work to do, Teddy?"

"Nothing much. I just came in to see if anyone else was here. How about you?"

"Not much. Just a couple of things and then I'm off to the gym again."

I slumped with disappointment before I remembered that I wasn't going to show emotion over every little thing.

So there was no chance of Devon walking me home today. Maybe tomorrow. Stay serene, I told myself.

"I guess I'll be going, then." I got up and made myself walk straight to the door without looking back, the way Fine did. Devon said good-bye as I closed the door behind me. If I hadn't promised myself that I was going to change my personality, I would have slammed the door hard enough to knock it off its hinges.

I caught up with Lucie and Jo-Sue about a block away from school. They were dawdling along, kicking at the leaves that littered the sidewalk. Neither of them looked very happy.

"How come you canceled the *Gazette* meeting? We always have one," I said to Lucie.

"There's plenty of time before the next issue comes out, and no one seemed to be in the mood for anything," Lucie said.

We poked along for half a block. "Why don't we get hot-fudge sundaes?" I suggested.

I can't," Lucie said sadly. "I have to give up chocolate until my allergies clear up."

"What a shame." The new Teddy wasn't much of a companion. At that rate, I decided, I might have Devon by Christmas, but everyone else would yawn when they saw me coming. "Actually, it's really awful. How about strawberry? There must be something you can eat."

Lucie shook her head. "If it's fun, I'm allergic to it."

The old Teddy would have said, "Come and eat health food at my house. Mom will love you." But the new Teddy just said "Hmmm."

"What do you suppose is going to happen to Billy?" Jo-Sue asked.

"Oh, everything will settle down pretty soon, and Trumpet will find out who really did it." That was me talking.

Both Lucie and Jo-Sue gawked at me. "When pigs can fly," Jo-Sue said.

My stomach was tied in knots, although I would have died before admitting it. My headache was worse. I wanted to jump up and down and yell that Trumpet was unfair. I wanted to draw a cartoon so devastating that Trumpet wouldn't be able to show his face outside his own house for a year.

But I also wanted to walk in the park with Devon again, hand in hand, listening to the wind rock the trees and watching the leaves blow around our feet. I wanted to be his steady girl, his steady, *quiet* girl. I wanted him to kiss me again.

Those wonderful things were more likely to happen if I could replace a few of Devon's memories of me. Right then he probably thought of me as the girl who got into noisy debates with Zack over everything. Teddy Gideon, the person most likely to give someone a nervous tic, couldn't compare in his mind with gentle, smiling Fine, who whispered in corners and needed sheltering.

After a few blocks Jo-Sue, Lucie, and I went our separate ways. I took my stomachache home to keep my headache company.

Chapter Seventeen

THURSDAY MORNING I caught a glimpse of Billy on my way to school. I was sure that he saw me too, but he didn't stop or wave.

I hadn't seen him for days, and I hadn't thought of him much because I'd been so busy perfecting the New Me. Now my conscience bothered me. I started to run to catch up to him, but then I changed my mind. If he got the wrong idea again, I'd be right back where I had started with him, and I'd have to explain all over again that we could only be friends.

"Darn it, anyway!" I was so frustrated that I was talking to myself. The New Me had to remind excitable old Teddy that the best thing I could do was nothing at all. Somehow everything would work out, and while it was working itself out, I was going to have to keep telling myself that I couldn't love someone just because he loved me. It would be cruel to give Billy false hopes.

Someday we'd end up being friends again.

The whole *Gazette* staff was in the office when I got there, and Fine and Devon were sitting together on one side of the table. I sat down opposite Fine, next to Zack, and he shoved half his cinnamon roll over to me.

"I saved this for you."

I thanked him and ate it, even though my stomach still bothered me. I wanted to kid him a little and ask him how many demerits he got for carrying the cinnamon roll from the cafeteria to our office, but that sort of thing wasn't something the new Teddy would say.

However, it would have distracted me from the sight of Devon sitting so close to Fine.

Lucie gave us her ideas for the next edition of the *Gazette* and asked if we had anything to add. The only one who seemed to have given any thought to the matter was Devon, so we all listened attentively.

Fine was listening a little too attentively. She looked as if she was working herself up into a coma. Her smile looked painted on, and she didn't even blink.

Did I really want to be like her?

Oh, Teddy, I thought. That wasn't the question. I should have been asking myself if I really wanted to attract Devon's attention to the point where he never looked at anyone else.

I did.

This was definitely not a brainstorming session. Usually, when we got together, ideas were flying all over, arguments were breaking out, and voices were raised as loudly as Lucie would allow. Lucie, of course, always sat back at her desk, watching and listening. She never really got involved, but she was always ready to make quiet final decisions.

This week had been different, and today was the worst. Lucie sat blowing her nose and not paying much attention to anything. Zack played with the crumbs he had scattered around the table. The twins fiddled endlessly with scraps of paper, and Fine looked up to smile at Devon occasionally. I just sat, trying to think of something—anything—to say that would be intelligent. My headache started up again.

"Well," Lucie said finally, "we don't seem ready to get going. What's the problem, gang?"

Everyone looked at me.

"What did I do?" I said.

They all looked at each other and then back at me. "You

116

always have something to say," Zack said. "What's the matter? We count on you."

"Sure," said Sure.

"It's true," Lucie said. "You have a way of setting off the rest of us, Teddy."

"We listen to see what you're going to say, and then we add to it," Devon said. "You're the spark that lights the fire."

Zack snorted and I gave him a cool look. I was trying to pretend that Devon hadn't given me goose bumps. I was also wondering if he really meant what he said. He might have meant that I was the one who usually did most of the talking, with some noisy encouragement from Zack, of course.

"You're imagining things," I told them. "It sounds to me as if everyone is fresh out of inspiration. Maybe we ought to visit Miss Bilky and get some ideas."

"Fine," murmured Fine. She looked at Devon for approval. "We could go after school."

"I've got a doctor's appointment." Lucie always had a doctor's appointment.

"I've got to cover football practice," Zack said.

"Oh." Fine looked disappointed until Devon smiled at her.

Lucie stood up. "Okay, gang. Let's try again tomorrow. And remember that everyone is responsible for ideas." She gave me a significant look.

The twins shot out the door, not looking back. Devon went to Lucie's desk for a private conference, so Zack and I left together.

We were halfway down the hall when he said, "Your new personality is the pits, Teddy. What are you trying to prove?"

"I don't know what you're talking about," I began angrily, and then I changed my tone of voice. "Have I offended you somehow?"

Zack hit his forehead with the flat of his hand. "That's exactly what I mean. You sound just like the twins. They never come right out and say something—they always talk at you sideways so that you don't really know what they think. Now you're doing it, too. Does this have something to do with the perfume you girls wear? Is it the dumb diets you all keep trying?"

"Zack," I interrupted. "Watch my lips. I don't know what you're talking about, and you don't either. Now bug off, will you?"

Zack grinned and pretended to mop his brow. "There's my Teddy! I knew you were in there somewhere."

I turned and walked away from him. Darn, I thought. If anyone could break down my resolve, it would be that crazy Zack, with his glasses with fingerprints on the lenses and crumbs decorating his sweater.

I almost made it to first period safely. If I'd had my wits about me, I would have been watching the people in the hall, but I had Devon on my mind, as usual, and so Trumpet caught me unprepared.

"Teddy Gideon!" he called out.

Everybody stared. I could feel a blush start at my neckline and flood my face. "Yes, Mr. Trumpteller?" I replied sweetly.

"I'd like to see you about that column."

I racked my brain and couldn't think of what he was talking about. "What column?" I asked. Out of the corner of my eye I saw Devon and Fine walking by, a little too close together for my taste. They both looked at me sympathetically.

Be cool, I told myself.

"The gossip column. It's falling flat. There's no life in it."

I nodded. So that's what this was all about. "Someone else used to do it and . . ."

"Don't you want to win an award this year?" Trumpet persisted. "You'll be letting the school down if you don't."

The hall was clearing out. I was going to be late again, and panic was setting in. "Of course we want to win, but I don't think the gossip column matters." I tried to edge away from him.

"Of course it matters! Everything matters. Where's your enthusiasm?"

"I'm trying," I explained carefully while I silently counted to ten.

"The column has to be jazzed up, if you know what I mean. Perhaps I'd better keep a closer watch on the *Gazette* until Miss Bilky returns."

That did it. My stomachache and headache joined forces and the old Teddy came roaring out. "I'm doing my best, but I'm not a gossip columnist! When we had a full staff, someone else wrote it. But we don't have a full staff now because of that dumb Student Justice Committee!"

Then, to my complete disgust, I burst into tears.

This man was driving me crazy. He seemed to think that the best place to settle problems was in the hall, where everyone could hear. How dare he criticize my work! I hated him — and I couldn't quit crying.

Trumpet's face turned an interesting shade of red. I'm sure that if the bell hadn't rung just then, I would have been in terrible trouble. But the instant the bell rang, I turned and ran. Luckily, he didn't call me back.

I couldn't concentrate on anything. I had been embarrassed again by that awful man. And to make things even worse, Devon and Fine had probably seen and heard everything. Any hope I'd had of convincing Devon I could be his ideal girl was in big trouble.

The more I thought about it, the angrier I got. I was nearly doubled up, my stomach hurt so much, and that must have been the reason I got the crazy idea.

I wouldn't even let myself think it over. I cut my next

class and headed straight for the art room, where I borrowed a big sheet of paper and a bottle of black ink from the art teacher.

Then, after checking to see that the hall monitors were patrolling somewhere else, I taped the paper to Trumpet's door and did the best cartoon I've ever done.

It took me only a few minutes. When I stepped back to admire my work, I couldn't help grinning, and my stomachache disappeared like magic. There was Trumpet—tall and uncoordinated, his mouth open from ear to ear and a balloon coming out of it with the words, "Nag, nag, nag!" No one would have any trouble recognizing him.

I bent down and drew my own personal teddy bear on the corner of the paper.

Then, still smiling, I went to my class, accepted demerits for being so late, and sat down. No matter what happened, I was willing to take my punishment. The only thing I was sorry about was that I wouldn't be able to see Trumpet's face when he came out of his office and saw my cartoon.

Drawing that cartoon was the worst thing I'd ever done in my life. I was sure that the great cosmic bad-luck machine already knew about it and was lining up overhead, ready to let me have it.

Two hours passed before Trumpet saw the cartoon. By then everyone else had looked it over and laughed, even some of the teachers.

Trumpet hauled me out of class, just as I expected. I was really scared. But he didn't look mad as much as he looked, well, hurt.

"Take the cartoon down," he said, sighing. "You'll be in penalty study hall for the rest of the semester."

I ripped the paper off the door without saying a word. It had been worth it. I wasn't even sorry that I might have hurt his feelings.

When I went to the *Gazette* office after school, the rest of the staff stood up and clapped. Even Devon. We spent our time talking about the cartoon and Trumpet's reaction, and afterward Devon walked home with me. I was surprised about that, since the new Teddy had failed totally.

"You'll have lots of company in the penalty study hall." He took my hand. "Try not to feel too bad."

"I'll try," I said demurely. The awful truth was that I didn't feel bad at all, since my headache and stomachache were gone.

"It was the best cartoon I've ever seen. Too bad you didn't save it."

"I'll do a better one," I said.

"For the paper?"

I laughed. "I don't think that's such a good idea. I may not be on the paper much longer if I don't behave."

It was a lovely walk. Devon did most of the talking, which was all right with me. His hand gripped mine firmly, and I felt secure. I suppose that was how Fine felt whenever Devon rescued her.

We were almost home when I saw Cal behind us. I turned my head just as he ducked behind a car, and I thought about mentioning him to Devon, then changed my mind. Cal was getting stranger all the time—I wasn't sure I wanted Devon to know about him. There was no way I could explain why Cal seemed to be following me. And he *was* following me. Whenever I could, I sneaked a look back and saw him half a block away, as persistent as an echo. I decided I'd better forget him, since there wasn't anything I could do.

Devon didn't come into the house, but I was satisfied that he'd walked me home. "I'll see you, Teddy," he said. The way he smiled at me made my heart turn over.

Dominic wanted out the back door the minute I came in. Mom was in the kitchen, reading as usual, and I didn't interrupt her to tell her what had happened in school. I wasn't sure she was ready for a story like that. Parents never are.

I put my jacket and books away, spent a few minutes looking at myself in the mirror—trying to see what Devon had seen—and then wandered downstairs again. Still daydreaming, I fixed Dominic's kibbles and went to the door to call him. He wasn't in the yard.

"Dominic got out again," I told Mom. "I suppose he's napping on the walk."

But he wasn't. I looked up and down the block, and Dominic was gone.

Chapter Eighteen

I COULDN'T FIND Dominic anywhere. After I had searched the neighborhood, including Mrs. Dimwitly's yard, Mom took the car and began driving up and down the streets, all the way to the business district.

It occurred to me that Dominic might have followed Devon home, so I called him.

"Hold on, Teddy," he said after I'd explained my problem. "Let me go outside and look."

I waited for what seemed like forever before Devon got back to the phone.

"I didn't see him anywhere. Listen, I'll come right back to your place, and I'll watch for him on my way. If I don't see him, I'll help you look."

I was so grateful I almost cried.

Dad came home and Mom got back from her drive. She hadn't seen Dominic, and she and Dad looked almost as upset as I was. We forgot all about dinner.

When Devon arrived, he and I decided to start out on foot, following the same route Mom had taken with her car. We thought perhaps Dominic was napping in some strange little hideaway that she hadn't seen when she drove by.

"While you're doing that, I'll go have a look at the pound," Dad offered.

"He won't be there. Not this soon," Mom protested. I

could tell she was hoping that Dominic would come wandering down the block any minute.

"I'll look anyway, but first I'm going to have a talk with that woman next door. For all we know, she might have called the pound and had him picked up." Dad went out, slamming the door behind him, and we decided not to follow and watch the fireworks.

He was back in minutes. "She is absolutely crazy."

"But did she have Dominic picked up?" Mom asked.

Dad shook his head. "I doubt it. She wouldn't want to risk their making a mistake and taking her instead."

He took off for the pound, and Devon and I started to retrace Mom's route. We looked down every driveway and over every fence. There wasn't an alley we didn't explore, and on every street we called Dominic's name.

We didn't find my dog. Devon and I walked home hand in hand in the dark, but I was too miserable to appreciate it.

"He'll turn up," Devon said, giving my hand an extra-hard squeeze. "Dogs do things like this."

"Not Dominic. He's never run off like this. Something bad has happened to him, I just know it."

I wanted to tell Devon about the great cosmic bad-luck machine, but I restrained myself. I was sure Fine didn't believe in stuff like that, and even though I was more scared than I'd ever been, I still wanted Devon to think that I was basically a very quiet, practical girl.

My folks were eating sandwiches in the kitchen when we got back to the house. Dad told us that Dominic wasn't at the animal shelter. Mom reported that she'd called everyone she knew to ask if Dominic might be hanging around some other neighborhood. No luck.

I fixed sandwiches for Devon and me, but neither of us wanted food. He finally went home about ten o'clock.

The house seemed big and quiet that night. I was so lonely for my dog that I cried myself to sleep.

Dominic didn't show up overnight, and when I walked to school, I kept watch for him. Devon met me at the intersection, looking worried.

"I can tell by your face that Dominic didn't come home," he said.

I must have been dragging one foot after the other, and that's not a pretty sight, but it didn't seem important that day. A thin, fine rain was falling, and I thought of Dominic getting wet and cold and hungry. It was all I could do to keep from running back home.

Everyone on the *Gazette* was sorry about my dog, everyone except Fine. She was home with a bad cold, Lucie told us.

"She sounded awful when I called her this morning," Devon volunteered. "But she came up with a couple of good ideas for the general news page."

If I hadn't been so worried about Dominic, that remark would have ruined my whole day. So he was calling her every morning? I'd feel devastated about that just as soon as I got my dog back.

Zack caught up with me on my way to my first class. He looked big and rumpled and safe, and for once I was glad to see him.

"I'll go home with you after school and help you look for Dominic," he told me. "I wish you'd called me last night. I would have been glad to help. But I'll make up for it now."

"Oh, Zack, there's no point. We looked everywhere."

Zack's nice, earnest face drew into a scowl. "Dogs are strange sometimes. He might have found another hideout and settled in there. It's important that you don't give up."

"I'll never give up!" I protested.

"Then I'll help you after school," Zack said. Suddenly he threw his arms around me and gave me an awkward hug.

125

I shoved him away. "For Pete's sake, Zack. It's *my* dog that's lost, not yours." I rushed away from him, embarrassed by his display of affection, or whatever it was. Zack hadn't hugged me since his mother made him do it at our Christmas party when we were in fourth grade.

That was a long day. I couldn't eat lunch, even though Jo-Sue kept urging all sorts of goodies on me. For once I was glad that lunchtime was over.

"Don't worry about Dominic," she told me. "He'll probably be home when you get there. And don't worry about what's going to happen to you at the next Student Justice Committee meeting. There's nothing on my list about sentencing anyone to a whole semester in penalty study hall. Trumpet has to obey his own rules."

I told her that our dear principal had given me practically a life sentence because of the cartoon. Somehow not even that seemed very important today.

Maybe I'd just do what Billy did—he never showed up for penalty study hall. I was willing to bet that he never would. And the world had not come to an end either, although the next sentence he got from the committee might be as long as mine.

I didn't see Billy at school all day, and I wondered what he would think when he learned that Dominic was missing. He had given the dog to me, and he loved him almost as much as I did.

I thought that Devon would be waiting for me in the *Gazette* office after school, ready to walk home with me. Don't ask me how I came up with that fantasy. He hadn't said one word about it. But after all, he had waited for me that morning, and the night before he had helped me look for Dominic.

During the day I managed to convince myself that in spite of his calling Fine first thing in the morning, he still

126

preferred my company. Desperation makes people silly, I guess.

"Devon took off right after sixth period to visit Fine," Lucie told me the minute I opened the *Gazette* office door. She was the only one in the office, and she looked genuinely sympathetic.

I stood there like a six-year-old who'd just found out that she wasn't going to be invited to a birthday party. I felt betrayed.

"I wasn't going to stay, anyway," I said finally. "I'm going to go home and look for Dominic again."

"I figured you would. We can manage without you. Good luck." Lucie blew me a kiss.

I left just as Zack was coming in with Sure right behind him.

"See you tomorrow," I said, trying not to sound as if I might start crying.

Zack called out something, but I didn't wait. I couldn't. If he had said one word to me about Devon, my heart would have broken.

The great cosmic bad-luck machine followed me home. Even though I had called Mom three times during the day to ask about Dominic, I still expected to see him in the front hall when I walked through the door. He wasn't there.

I changed into my oldest clothes and went out into the rain. Maybe Dominic was in the park somewhere, hurt. I was determined to search every inch of it, although Mom had told me she'd driven around it half a dozen times during the day.

It's not such a big park, but it was nearly dark before I finished poking through the shrubbery. I even crawled under the bandstand and got spider webs in my hair. A fat, fuzzy white dog started following me after a while, and he was joined by a brown poodle and an old beagle wearing a red leather collar. They didn't know where Dominic was either.

I took the long way home, stopping by Billy's house. I figured he might have heard about Dominic's disappearance from someone, and maybe he had some ideas. And if he hadn't heard yet, I wanted to be the one who told him.

Mr. McGill answered the door and called Billy out of his room. Billy hadn't heard about Dominic, and telling him was hard to do.

"How long has Dominic been gone?" Billy asked. He sounded hoarse, and he looked a little pale, too.

"Since yesterday. Are you all right, Billy? You look awful."

He shook his head irritably. "I caught whatever Cal had, but I'm lots better now. I'll get my jacket and we can go look for our dog."

He turned and would have left the room, but I grabbed his arm. "Billy, I've looked everywhere. There isn't any place I haven't been. Dad went to the animal shelter twice, and Mom drove through every street in Catherwood. Dominic's gone."

Billy looked stricken. "He can't be. He's got to be somewhere, and we're going to find him."

"Do you suppose that someone might have taken him?" I asked. That idea had been lurking around in the back of my mind all day, and Billy was the only person I felt I could mention it to.

"It's possible," he said. "But Dominic is only a mixed-breed dog. He isn't worth anything. If he were really valuable, then . . ."

"I was thinking about something else," I said hesitantly.

Billy shook his head, reading my mind. "He's too old to be dognapped by one of those creeps who sells dogs for medical experiments. And he's much too big."

I needed to hear Billy say that. I was so relieved that I

128

sagged against him, and he put his arms around me. "We'll find Dominic, Teddy. Don't worry about it anymore. We really will find him."

"But I don't know where to look now," I protested, pulling away.

Billy had a funny look on his face. "I'm not sure I do either. But I'll borrow my dad's car tonight, and then again tomorrow morning, before it gets light. I've heard that stray dogs are more likely to move around in the late evening or early morning when there are fewer people on the streets."

"I'm going with you!"

Billy shook his head. "No. You're worn out. Let me do this my way."

Billy didn't look well enough to do all he said he would. But I was grateful for his help, even though by that time I didn't think that Dominic would ever be found.

Billy took me home in his dad's car, and when he dropped me off he told me once more not to worry. Ha.

Zack had called several times while I was gone, but I was too tired to talk to anyone. I went to my room and sat by the window, hoping that Dominic would come trotting down the street.

And I hoped that Devon would call to find out if my dog was back. He cared the night before. Now—nothing. I truly did not know what he thought of me. One moment he seemed interested and caring, and the next he didn't know I was alive unless I stood right in front of him. Already he'd forgotten how much my dog meant to me. What kind of friend would do that?

Dad knocked on my bedroom door. "Zack is on the phone again. He says he's sorry about Dominic and wants to know if you'd like to go out for pizza with him."

Good old Zack. He remembered that food usually cheered me up, but this time I was too scared to eat.

"Tell him no thanks," I said.

Winter dark is different from summer dark. There's something terrible and lonely about it. If my dog was still alive, he was out there, cold and alone, wondering why I didn't come to make things right for him.

I was inside where it was warm, and there was no one in the world who could make things right for me that night.

Chapter Nineteen

I WOKE UP at dawn, so cold and stiff that you'd have thought I was the one lost in the night with no place to sleep. The first thing I did was go to my window and look out.

The birch trees in the yard had lost most of their leaves by then, and moisture was beaded on the bare twigs like crystals strung on threads. The empty street glistened. Billy and Dominic were out there somewhere, and I hoped they weren't too far apart. Billy had promised to find my dog, and I believed he could.

The house was so quiet I could hear the clock ticking in the downstairs hall. I dressed and went back to the window.

I think my heart heard Billy's car before I did, because I was halfway down the stairs before my mind told me why I was running. A car was coming down the street, still out of sight, but coming. And it had to be Billy's.

I was out on the porch by the time he pulled up and stopped. I froze on the top step, both hands pressed against my mouth. Billy opened the car door, and my big, dumb, wonderful dog plopped out and waddled toward me.

He was wet and dirty, but I didn't care. I hugged him while he lapped my face with his rough tongue, and I didn't care that Billy saw me crying either.

"He's okay," Billy said. "He's just cold and tired. And hungry too, I bet."

"Where did you find him?" Dominic was leaning against me so hard that I nearly fell over. My clothes were muddy, but that didn't matter. Nothing mattered now.

Billy didn't answer, and I looked up at him, surprised. "Where was he?" I asked again. Suddenly, I wasn't so sure that I wanted to hear the answer.

"He was up at the Last Mile Point picnic grounds."

"How could Dominic have gotten that far? He's never even seen the place, and it's miles from here."

Billy's face looked white and sick. "Cal took him there. He tied him up with a rope and led him up there."

For a moment I was speechless. Poor old Dominic. He trusted everyone. He wouldn't have resisted. He had been at the picnic grounds all that time, cold and alone.

"Why?" I shouted. "Why would Cal do such a rotten thing?"

Billy rubbed one hand over his eyes. "I hauled him out of bed in the middle of the night and made him tell me. I'd been wondering if maybe he wasn't the one who was helping Dominic get out of the yard. And when I added everything up—all the other trouble he's been in, I mean —well, it made sense to me that he was the one responsible."

"What other trouble? What are you talking about?"

Billy's eyes were huge and haunted. "Hey, can we sit down on the porch? I'm really tired."

"Let's go into the house," I said quickly. Billy looked as if he were ready to drop.

But he shook his head. "I'm not ready to face your folks."

"You didn't do anything! It was Cal! And what did you mean, 'other trouble'?"

We sat together on the porch, with Dominic close beside me, and Billy covered the dog with his jacket.

"Cal's the one who's been vandalizing the parking lot at

132

school," Billy began. "He's been expelled from the junior high now. He's done a lot of stuff, and he's in big trouble."

"But why would he try to hurt my dog?"

Billy shook his head. "It's not that he wanted to hurt Dominic. He wanted to hurt you."

I stared at Billy. "I've never done anything to Cal. It doesn't make sense."

Billy looked down at his feet. "He didn't like seeing you with Devon. And he knew that Zack came here for dinner. I guess he watches you a lot."

"But why? He's just a kid. Why does he care who I see?"

Billy couldn't meet my eyes. "He thought you should be my girl, so he punished you when things didn't work out. I'm sorry. I shook him until he told me everything. You've got to understand that Cal has lots of problems. Serious ones. And that's why Dad is sending him to Seattle to live with our aunt. Cal can go to a special school there and get help. So you don't need to worry anymore. He'll be gone by next weekend."

I tried to digest all this information at once, but it was too much for me. "I can't believe this has happened," I said. "Does Trumpet know that Cal was the one who did all those things?"

Billy nodded. "Sure. He caught Cal the last time he tried something. Before that, he thought it was me."

I touched Billy's arm. "I'm so sorry. This must have been awful for you."

"I can handle it."

I considered something for a moment. "I don't suppose your dad knows yet about Cal hiding Dominic."

"No. He wasn't awake when I left, but I'll tell him when I get back."

"Billy, look at me for a minute," I said quietly, and Billy raised his face.

"Thank you for telling me. You could have just said you found Dominic accidentally."

He looked away again. "I know."

We sat for a moment without speaking, and then Billy said, "You and Dominic had better get into the house. Both of you need a hot breakfast. And rub him dry first."

I stood, and Dominic waddled up the steps. "Billy, I'll never be able to thank you enough for this."

Billy started down the steps, his hands in his pockets and that familiar half-smile on his face. "Go on inside."

"But . . ."

Billy waved to me and got into his dad's car. He drove away without looking back.

Dominic was waiting at the door for me, patiently wagging his tail. I let him in and looked down the street once more. The car was gone.

"Billy," I whispered, "I'm so sorry."

We gave Dominic a rubdown with Mom's best towels. While she was drying his long fur with her hair dryer, Dad fixed Dominic what he called a proper breakfast — bacon, eggs, pancakes, and toast. I tried to make Dad understand that all that food would probably make Dominic sick since he hadn't eaten for a long time, but Dad insisted on fixing enough food to feed an army. I guess it made him feel better.

But Dominic had more sense than to eat much. He nibbled a piece of toast, then lumbered upstairs and crawled up on my bed. I followed and saw that he was asleep in an instant. On his back. Life was almost back to normal.

I went to see Miss Bilky that afternoon and found her anxious to return to school.

"Even with the Student Justice Committee spoiling everything?" I asked her.

"Have patience," she told me. "Once the rough edges

are worn off, you may find it bearable. You might even find Mr. Trumpteller bearable."

"Never," I said. "His edges are too rough. He kills flies by running over them with a truck. Somebody has to do something about him."

"Make sure *you* don't try killing flies with a truck," Miss Bilky warned. "Just wait. Things have a way of working out."

But both of us knew I didn't believe that.

Zack and Devon got off the hospital elevator just as I got on. "Wait for us," Zack begged. "We'll stay for a few minutes and then catch up with you in the snack bar. I called your house and your dad said that Dominic was back. We should celebrate."

Devon held open the elevator door and grinned at me. "Is he okay?"

"He's fine, but I can't wait for you. I've got things to do."

Devon let go of the elevator door as Zack started to say something. Well, he'd call later if it was important. I needed time alone to think.

As I walked away from the hospital, I realized that if Devon actually cared about me, he would have been the one to suggest that I meet them in the snack bar, not Zack. I was wasting my time—always longing to see him and looking for ways to run into him. It was like giving a party and no one showing up. Over and over and over.

Dominic was awake when I got home, sharing a hamburger with Dad.

"I heard today that Cal is moving to Seattle," Dad said, scowling at me as if it were all my fault.

"I was going to tell you. I guess I just needed time to adjust to the idea."

Dad gave Dominic the last of the burger. "I ran into his father downtown. He told me he's had quite a bit of trouble with the boy."

"That's what I heard." I could have told him that Cal was the one who hid Dominic away from us for that endless, awful time, but I didn't. Not that I owed Cal anything. But I owed Billy.

That night Jo-Sue, Lucie, and I went to a movie, and guess who we saw? Devon. He was with another boy from the track team. Devon waved at us and smiled. And my dumb, stubborn heart was glad that he wasn't with Fine. Maybe, in spite of everything, if I were patient, and if I didn't try to force anything, Devon would discover that I was worth more attention than he'd ever paid me.

But I was done arranging things. Too much had happened to me in the last few days. I was worn out with trying to make things turn out right.

Chapter Twenty

"THEODORA, MY LOVE, this is for you." Zack dropped a greasy paper bag on the table in front of me and sat down, grinning.

"What's in it? A bomb?" The rest of the *Gazette* staff laughed, but I was in no mood to join in. The Tuesday mornings before the paper came out could be hectic, and this was one of the worst.

"It looks edible," Lucie said from her desk. "I hope you brought enough to share, Zack."

Since everyone was waiting, I opened the bag. Doughnuts, from the horrid little shop across the street. If I was going to be polite and eat one, I'd be in no mood to eat Mom's Peanut-and-Brussel-Sprout Surprise at lunch. After all, how much gourmet food can we consume in one day?

"Thank you, Zack." I helped myself and shoved the sack down the table to Fine. She turned pale and passed the bag to Sure.

Zack leered at me over the rims of his glasses. "Don't say I never did anything special for you."

I bit into my doughnut, then bent my head over my cartoon. It was finished, but I still wasn't happy with it. Maybe I wasn't satisfied because Trumpet would think it was great. I'd drawn a really silly cartoon of one of the football players hobbling down the hall on crutches, followed by Miss Bilky, who was also hobbling along on crutches. A player had broken his leg the Saturday before, and Miss Bilky was leaving the hospital at the end of the week. Big joke.

I really wanted to draw the main hall, immaculate and empty, with a big vending machine outside the office door and a sign on the machine: DEMERITS. TAKE ONE.

Lucie interrupted my brooding. "I heard that Billy McGill's brother is leaving town."

"Billy is awfully cute," Fine said thoughtfully.

She had my undivided attention. Fine thought *Billy* was cute? Could she possibly think Billy was cuter than Devon? Was there a way I could encourage her interest in Billy and maybe solve two of my problems at once?

No, that was impossible. No one in the whole world was as attractive as Devon. Of course, with a little help from the good old cosmic bad-luck machine, Fine would probably end up with both Devon and Billy, and I wouldn't even get Zack, because twice now I'd seen him openly flirting with a red-haired cheerleader. And she had been flirting back. Not that I minded, exactly. Well, maybe a little bit.

Devon and Sure had been passing sheets of paper back and forth, and now Devon handed his to Lucie. "We're ready. If everyone else is too, why don't we cut the meeting after school and all go out instead?"

Zack leaped up. "We can leave right from school. I've got my car."

"You do not have your car," I told him. "The student parking lot's still closed. Your car is home, like everyone else's."

Zack strutted around the room while Devon, obviously knowing his secret, laughed. "I brought it and parked it in the faculty lot," Zack said finally.

I put my head down on the table and groaned. "Tell me you're kidding."

"He is definitely not kidding. I saw him do it. He parked in Miss Bilky's spot," Devon said.

"We'll seek alternate means of transportation," Lucie said solemnly.

"Why?" Zack cried. "I even washed the old bus this weekend."

"Mr. Trumpteller will have it towed away, that's why."

Zack stared at Lucie as if he had never seen her before. "He wouldn't do that. He won't even notice it."

As if it had all been planned, the door opened, slamming against the wall, and Trumpet leaped into the room.

"Young man!" he shouted at Zack. "Can't you read? 'ALL UNAUTHORIZED VEHICLES WILL BE IMPOUNDED.' That's what the sign says. Now get your car out of the faculty lot!"

The bell rang and Zack turned pale. "I'll be late for my first-period class if I have to move my car now!"

"You should have thought of that before you broke the rules." Trumpet stalked out, leaving the door open.

"If I get any more demerits, I'll be in penalty study hall for sure," Zack moaned.

"Join the club," I told him. Believe me, I felt no pity for him at all. He knew he had broken the rules, and he must have been crazy to think he could get away with it. Everyone knew his ugly old car by sight.

Zack finally decided to deal with his problem instead of lurching around the room complaining. He took off, practically at the speed of light, and the rest of us gathered up our stuff and filed out into the hall.

There it was. Trumpet's Paradise. The hall was so clean we could have walked on it with white socks. No one was yelling. There was no pushing and shoving on the stairs. And the monitors seemed to blend into the background now. Catherwood High was surviving, but I took no pleasure in the fact. I hated Trumpet's getting results like this because his methods were all wrong.

Devon wandered along beside me for the length of the hall, laughing about Zack and talking easily about where we might go after school. My heart thumped the whole time and I didn't look up at his profile. I hoped, even though I knew better, that he'd say something really personal to me like, "Teddy, I've finally made up my mind. You're the girl I want."

He didn't. In fact, at the end of the hall he spotted Beth Kirk, called out her name, and took off after her.

"See you later," was all that he called back to me.

Meanly, I hoped he would miss second bell and be late to class.

After school Zack retrieved his car from the side street where he'd parked it that morning, and we drove through a nasty rainstorm to a wonderful Chinese restaurant. We were too late for lunch and too early for dinner, but the waiters knew us and gave us a special table in an alcove. We had a good time until just before we were getting ready to leave.

I saw Billy and Cal before anyone else did, and the smile on my face began to hurt. Billy's dad came in after them, looking awfully depressed, and the three of them sat at a table on the other side of the room.

One by one, the *Gazette* people saw the McGills, and the laughter at our table died down. Even though I'd hoped no one would find out about Cal, everyone knew.

"Well, gang, I guess we'd better fold up this party and get going," Zack said uneasily. He signaled the waiter for our checks, and my eyes blurred with tears. His big strong hand gripped my arm and he propelled me out the restaurant door. The others followed quietly and Zack drove us home.

Zack walked me from his car to the porch. He knew how sorry I felt for Billy. I guess he did too, because he cleared his throat hard and said, "Darn it, anyway." Then, to my astonishment, he bent and kissed me right on the mouth. "Stop your bawling, Teddy," he said. "Dominic will think I did something awful to you and kill me."

How could I help but laugh?

I was home barely ten minutes when Jo-Sue called.

"I've been trying to catch you ever since sixth period. I want to tell you what I did this afternoon."

"Okay. I'm listening." I sat down on the chair next to the phone, and Dominic flopped at my feet. He could tell that this would be a long call.

"I gave Trumpet's secretary my letter of resignation."

"You really did it? What did he say?"

"I don't know if he's even read it yet." Jo-Sue sounded depressed.

"What did you say in the letter?" I asked.

I could hear paper being unfolded. "I made a copy of it during fifth period. I wrote, 'I am resigning from my office of president of the junior class because I have strong moral objections to serving on the Student Justice Committee. The committee is unjust because the students are not allowed to defend themselves. They do not have representation, and their accusers are not present. The judges do not serve willingly, and therefore they are being punished as unfairly as the students. Furthermore, the publication of the students' names in the *Gazette* represents an invasion of their privacy and is offensive to everyone.'"

"Wow," I breathed, impressed. "That says it all."

"I don't care how mad Trumpet gets," Jo-Sue said. "The committee is just not fair! He carps about rules and regulations, and then he makes up his own as he goes along."

"Gee," I said, struck with a new idea. "This would make a great story for the *Gazette.*"

"I hope you print it! I mean it."

We talked for a while longer, but I couldn't get what Jo-Sue said out of my mind. After we hung up, I went to my room to think.

141

Tomorrow was the last day I could make changes on the feature page. There was time to do a new cartoon—one of the sassy teddy-bear cartoons. I could slip it in, replacing the old one, just before Zack went to the printer.

I went downstairs only once during the evening to get milk and crackers from the kitchen.

"Lots of homework tonight?" Dad asked as I walked through the living room.

"Some," I told him. "Mostly, I just had a great idea for a cartoon."

"It's nice having a genius for a daughter," Dad said.

"Don't stay up too late," Mom reminded me.

I went back to my desk. The cartoon was taking shape, and I was really pleased with it.

I drew the main hall with the vending machine. There was an open door at the end of the hall, and through the door you could see a long, empty room—the penalty study hall. The only person in it was Mr. Trumpteller.

He'd boil me in oil.

Even worse, Miss Bilky might be angry with me. I knew she wanted me to be patient. Yes, Trumpet was right about setting rules and cleaning up the school. But he was absolutely wrong about the Student Justice Committee. Maybe he didn't realize how unfair it was. Maybe he needed me, Teddy Gideon, to show him that he was dealing with real, live human beings who wanted respect just as much as he did.

I worked until late, showered, and got ready for bed. After I turned out the light, I went to the window.

The rain had stopped sometime during the evening, but I hadn't noticed because I was so busy. I looked out at the trees, illuminated by the streetlight, and saw that half the leaves were gone now. Spring was a long way off.

Billy stood under the streetlight, hands in his pockets, watching my house. My heart turned over. I could have opened my window and called out his name. I could have invited him in for hot chocolate in the kitchen. Maybe we could have talked the way we used to when we were kids. But Billy turned abruptly and hurried away into the dark at the end of the street. The opportunity was gone.

We would never have one of our talks again, because we were growing up too different from each other. And Billy knew that also.

It was late now, so when the phone rang, I didn't think it would be for me. But Dad knocked on my door a moment later. "Are you awake? Someone's on the phone for you."

I took the call on the upstairs extension.

"Teddy? It's Zack. Listen, I'm sorry to bother you so late, but I heard that Jo-Sue is resigning as class president. Did you know that?"

I swallowed hard. I didn't want him to know that I'd been crying. "She called me earlier."

"I think we ought to do something about it. The *Gazette* gang, I mean. I called Devon, because he's general news editor, but he said we'd better lie low on this one. What do you think? Should I call Lucie?"

"Let's leave Lucie out of it," I said quickly. "This is her last year, and there's no point in fouling things up for her." My tears dried as ideas flashed and fizzed in my mind. "I've already done a cartoon, and I was going to substitute it for my old one tomorrow, without telling you. Now, though..."

"I knew I could count on you!" Zack said. "Devon is the world's biggest coward. But listen, maybe we should call Fine."

"What for? She doesn't think without getting Devon's permission first."

"Aha! Then you haven't heard the latest."

I sat down on the floor and Dominic sprawled next to me. "What latest? I know everything that goes on."

"You don't know that Fine's nose is out of joint because Devon has been walking Beth home." Zack sounded triumphant. "She said Devon must get in shape for track by running circles around girls." Zack's big bray of laughter nearly broke my eardrum.

I thought about it and began laughing myself. "What did you have in mind?"

"How about Fine doing a small bit on Jo-Sue's resignation? Maybe reprinting her letter. We'll run it on the first page with a headline and maybe a picture of Jo-Sue."

"Ouch," I said. "Do you think Fine will get involved?"

"There's only one way to find out," Zack said. "Let's call and ask her."

I leaned back against the wall. "Zack, I think we're going to put out an edition that will wake up everybody."

"Or get our heads cut off at high noon in the main hall." He didn't sound as if he cared.

"Maybe," I said. "And maybe not. But no matter what happens, we'll have done what needed doing."

"Yeah," Zack said happily. Then, suddenly, his voice changed. "Teddy, I feel bad about Cal, too. I can't get him out of my mind."

I was hoping that no one would ever remind me. "It's so sad, Zack."

"I could see how upset you were at the restaurant."

I couldn't tell him that I'd just seen Billy outside our house. Zack would probably say I'd imagined him there. "Well, I've known Cal and Billy for a long time," I said.

There was a funny sort of silence on the line. I could almost hear the wheels in Zack's head turning. "Teddy?"

"I'm still here."

"Billy isn't your only old pal. I've known you as long as he has." His voice cracked. "I guess I've given you a hard time every chance I got. But I never wanted to hurt you or really make you mad at me. It's just that . . . Teddy, you're so darned smart, and so cute. I love to argue with you! It's like having a battle of wits, only nobody ever really gets hurt. Do you know what I mean?"

Good grief. Zack was going sentimental on me again.

"Zack, for Pete's sake, pull up your socks and quit that. We've got work to do, and this is no time to start talking over old times. You call Fine, and I'll call Sure. She'll want to help if her twin does, and we'll put out a paper that will shake up the school."

I wouldn't have dared let Zack know that his speech had brought tears to my eyes. He'd never spoken like that to me before, except when we were little kids and he told me I could balance on the top of a roof as long as a boy.

Zack cleared his throat noisily. "Right. I'll call Fine as soon as we hang up. And Teddy—forget what I said. Or what I almost said. We're pals, right? I wouldn't want you to be mad."

"I'll forget it," I assured him. But I wouldn't. I was too grateful to forget a single word.

After he hung up, I leaned over and gave Dominic a big hug. Then I jumped up and ran to my room for my note pad and telephone book. It was late, but I felt terrific. I had a plan for the feature page and some ideas for the front page. Who cared if the great cosmic bad-luck machine was waiting around for new opportunities?

The next days and weeks were certainly going to be interesting. And together Zack and I were going to stir things up. Maybe we couldn't change the world, but we could sure make some changes in our own small piece of it. And when the going got rough, I knew absolutely and positively that Zack would never walk off and let me fight the battle alone.

Chapter Twenty-one

"I'M GLAD I got you an orchid instead of the roses you wanted." Zack and I were sitting across the table from each other, holding hands and grinning.

The spring dance was a big success. The gym was crowded, and we had a real-live band, paid for by a fund-raising campaign the *Gazette* staff started right after Christmas.

When Zack came to the house to pick me up, he was so dressed up that my dad didn't recognize him for a moment. I was wearing the most gorgeous dress I'd ever owned, and Zack was right. The pale green orchid he'd given me was exactly right with my gold, glittery dress. I felt like a movie star.

We scarcely had a moment alone after we arrived because all my friends stopped by our table to congratulate me. It was the best night of my life.

Jo-Sue, late because her date couldn't tell time, came up and threw her arms around me. "I heard the news this afternoon. You're going to be the new managing editor of the *Gazette!* Congratulations! It's wonderful."

She and her date found seats farther down the table, and Zack and I were finally more or less alone. "I was afraid you'd turn the job down," Zack said.

"I almost did. I kept thinking about how much fun I had as feature editor. And then I wondered if Trumpet and Miss

146

Bilky came up with the idea of my being managing editor just to put an end to all the cartoons."

Zack laughed. "Little do they know. You'll find even more time to do cartoons when you're the big boss."

"Last fall I would never have believed this could happen," I said. "That was the worst time of my life."

Zack squeezed my hand. "Aren't you glad I talked you out of quitting the paper after that big flap about Jo-Sue's letter to Trumpet?"

I smiled at him. "I'm glad, but if you remind me one more time, I'll reconsider."

"No, you won't. You didn't really want to quit."

I didn't argue with him. Zack hadn't been in Trumpet's office while our principal flayed me alive. Jo-Sue's letter had appeared on the front page, and Trumpet immediately suspected that I was responsible.

My extra-special cartoon had had its effect, too. While I was standing in Trumpet's office, red-faced, angry, and wringing my hands, he'd turned to the feature page.

"That's how you really see me, isn't it?" he asked. He shoved the paper at me.

The cartoon had turned out better than I'd hoped. There Trumpet sat, all alone in the penalty study hall. Even though the drawing of him was quite small, I'd caught enough of his posture and build to make him clearly recognizable. I was proud of my work, but terrified of what he might do to me.

Trumpet took the paper back and studied it for a long time, then sighed. "You have created quite an incident."

"No. I commented on the incident *you* created," I replied quietly.

That was it. That's all we said. I left his office, planning to quit the paper, and I lived in fear for days. I showed up at the Student Justice Committee, where the junior-class vice-president was sitting in for Jo-Sue, to accept my pen-

147

alty. And for the rest of the semester, I sat for one hour every morning in a room with the other Catherwood criminals. Zack sat right behind me. Both of us survived.

But the Student Justice Committee didn't. When the second semester began, the committee was abandoned.

But not the demerit system. Only now, Trumpet took care of adding up the demerits and handing out punishment—in the form of short suspensions, and only for the worst of rule infractions.

We certainly didn't learn to love Trumpet, but we didn't hate him anymore. And privately, *very* privately, I felt sorry for him. I knew how it felt to make an idiot out of yourself.

Zack and I spent so much time together, in school and out, that after a while everyone thought of us as a couple, and I guess we did, too. I knew Zack would take me to the spring dance, even before he asked me. And I bet he knew I wanted to go with him.

We danced most of the dances, and both of us went back to the buffet table for seconds. We stood in line behind Devon and his date, the star runner on the girls' track team.

"So you're the new general manager of the *Gazette*," Devon said to me. "When my training schedule eases up, maybe I'll be around to see you guys."

"Fine handles all the stuff you used to do, so we're making her position permanent," I told him, helping myself to salad. I couldn't resist. Devon seldom showed up at the *Gazette* office but expected, I suppose, that we'd just sit there and wait for him to remember us. I don't think he liked finding out that we were surviving without him.

After we finished eating, I was expecting the band to start up again, but instead there was a long silence. Everyone looked at me.

"What's going on?" I asked Zack.

"Wait and see." He looked around impatiently.

Then Lucie and Miss Bilky came in through the door to

148

the hall, pushing a cart in front of them. There was a birthday cake on it, with lighted candles, and everyone began singing "Happy Birthday."

To me.

"You did this!" I cried to Zack.

He pulled off his glasses and leaned over to kiss me. "Happy birthday and congratulations, Teddy."

"But my birthday isn't until tomorrow, and you know I hate fusses!"

"That's why we had so much fun planning this."

Jo-Sue and Miss Bilky both hugged me, and Jo-Sue whispered in my ear, "It's really because you were the one who was never afraid to do what was right."

"Was everybody in on this?" I asked her.

She laughed. "No. Just your very best friends. We didn't think it would be very smart to make an all-school thing out of it. Sometimes victory celebrations have to be a little bit private. At least if you don't want to fight the war all over again."

We didn't get back to my house until one o'clock in the morning, and both Zack and I were exhausted.

He pulled me to him and kissed me. "Am I still invited to your house for dinner tomorrow? I'm crazy about birthday cake, and your mom swore she wouldn't make one out of bran and turnip tops."

"Of course you're invited!" He kissed me again. I liked it so much that I would have stayed out there for a long, long time, but Dominic had heard Zack's voice and was moaning on the other side of the door. "I've got to go in," I said. "I don't need to tell you again how beautiful the orchid is, and you know what a wonderful time I had."

Zack still held me. "Don't tell me, show me."

He kissed me once more, but by that time Dominic was howling, so we said good night.

Dominic followed me upstairs, yawning and complaining. My parents were in bed, so I turned out the hall lights behind us.

But I didn't turn on my bedroom light. I went straight to the window and looked out into the spring night. Zack's car was gone and the street was empty. The moon silvered new leaves on the trees, and when I pushed open my window, I could smell lilacs. I might have stood there for an hour with Dominic beside me resting his chin on the window sill. He was enjoying the night as much as I was.

Suddenly Dominic began whining deep in his throat. His shaggy tail swung back and forth.

Then I heard the sound of footsteps coming down the block. I leaned out the window, curious to see who was walking on our street so late at night.

It was Billy, moving toward my house with that easy stride I remembered. I waited until he was standing across from our porch, and then I called his name.

He looked up, startled.

"Wait for me. I'm coming down," I called softly, and Dominic and I ran for the stairs. I was out the door so fast that I left Dominic panting behind. This was the first time Billy had come by my house for a long time.

He grabbed me and swung me around, laughing. Dominic caught up with us then, and Billy had to put me down for a moment while he hugged our silly dog.

"What are you doing here?" I asked him. "I hardly ever see you these days, even at school."

We crossed the street together and sat on my porch, with Dominic at our feet. "I couldn't forget your birthday," Billy said.

"Our birthday," I corrected.

"Our birthday. I took a chance that you'd be home from the dance by now. I was going to throw a rock at your window to wake you up if you'd already gone to bed." He dug through his pockets and pulled out a small box. "Happy birthday, Teddy."

150

He handed the box to me. When I opened it, I saw a tiny gold locket on a chain as fine as thread. I lifted the locket and it gleamed under the streetlight. "Oh, Billy, it's beautiful."

"It opens," he said.

I tried to find the tiny catch so I could open the locket and see what it contained, but Billy stopped me. "I want you to wait until you're alone."

I could tell that this was important to him, so I nodded. "But can't you come in for a while?" I asked him.

"I don't want to wake up your folks. And I can't stay long. I wanted to see you one last time, Teddy."

"What do you mean, 'one last time'?"

"Dad is taking Cal and me to California."

"California! But why?"

"There's a hospital there for kids like Cal."

"You mean he isn't getting any better? I thought he was going to a special school in Seattle."

Billy was quiet for a long time. "It's not working out the way we'd hoped."

"But do you have to go, too?" All of a sudden it had sunk in that one of my oldest friends was going away and I would probably never see him again.

"I want to be with my family. Cal and Dad need me now." He stood up then and pulled me to my feet. "I've got to go, Teddy. Promise you'll take care of our dog."

"Oh, Billy!" I hugged him as hard as I could.

"And promise me that you'll take care of yourself, too," he said. He pulled my arms loose from around my neck. "Teddy, say good-bye."

"I don't think I can," I told him.

But he was moving away from me then. With one last pat on Dominic's big head, Billy turned toward the street.

"Billy!" I called.

But he didn't look back.

Dominic followed me inside the house, then marched past me toward the back door, his head down, as though he hoped that if he went into the backyard, his secret conspirator would be there to let him loose again. But Cal was gone now, so I called Dominic to come upstairs with me.

As I reached the head of the stairs, the phone rang. I snatched it up quickly, before it could wake my parents. For some crazy reason I thought it might be Billy, telling me he'd changed his mind and wasn't going away after all.

But it was Zack. "I couldn't go to sleep without saying good night to you one more time," he said, sounding embarrassed.

I cleared my throat and wiped the tears from my face. "You're a real character, Zack. You woke me up."

"You answered the phone too fast for that," he argued. "What were you up to?"

I squeezed the little velvet box in my hand tightly. "I was thinking about old friends," I said truthfully.

"And what did you decide about old friends?"

"Well, I guess that some old friends aren't a bit like us, and I don't know how they ever got to be our friends. But with others, we're friends because we're so much alike. And then there isn't all that pain. Maybe we get mad at each other, and maybe we even do a lot of yelling. But we can't break each other's hearts."

"I won't break your heart, Teddy," Zack whispered.

"I know."

"And we're more than old friends now."

"I know that, too. Is that why you called me? To tell me things I already know?"

Zack laughed. "No. I called you to ask you something that I didn't ask you when I said good night."

"What?" I asked suspiciously. With Zack, it could be anything.

There was a little pause. "Teddy, would you mind awfully much if I loved you? Sort of. A little bit, anyway."

I pressed the velvet box against my heart. "No, I wouldn't mind. That would be all right, I guess."

"Good! I figured it might be, because Devon is going with someone else, and—"

"Zack!" I shouted. "Will you quit before you ruin this romantic moment? If you go on much longer, you'll be telling me that I'm lucky to have you because my feet are so big."

"Actually—"

"Zack!"

He was laughing. "I'm the lucky one, Teddy. There's no one else like you."

After we finally hung up, I went to my room again. This time I turned on the light. I took the locket out of its box and pried it open carefully.

Tears filled my eyes, and I wiped them away. The locket contained two tiny pictures, one of Billy and the other of me, taken when we were little kids. I turned the locket over. Engraved on the back were the words BEST FRIENDS.

For always, I thought. I put the locket back in its box and slipped it under the scarves in the bottom drawer of my dresser. Then I unpinned the orchid Zack had given me and put it on the top of my dresser, where I would see it first thing in the morning.

Good-bye, Billy, I thought.

Good night, Zack.

JEAN THESMAN lives near Seattle with her family and several dogs.